**She took off her gardening gloves
and walked over to Tomas.
"So you fight your own battles, right?"**

She saw the resigned expression shuttering his
eyes and felt that strange tugging inside her
heart again. His eyes caught hers, and Callie
saw a barough him
like a bla   "That's
what I d   s dark hair
shimmer   ut…I want
you to pl   tter what,
can you do that.

She wanted to laugh at that suggestion. She
didn't trust easily, not since her husband had left
her, in the middle of a health crisis. Not since
she'd decided to live her life free and clear and
without any regrets. She trusted in the Lord.
That was her kind of trust.

"Sorry, I'm not so good at trusting these days."

This time, she was the one to walk away.

Books by Lenora Worth

LENORA WORTH

has written more than forty books for three different publishers. Her career with Love Inspired Books spans close to fifteen years. In February 2011 her Love Inspired Suspense novel *Body of Evidence* made the *New York Times* bestseller list. Her very first Love Inspired title, *The Wedding Quilt,* won *Affaire de Coeur*'s Best Inspirational for 1997, and *Logan's Child* won an *RT Book Reviews* Best Love Inspired for 1998. With millions of books in print, Lenora continues to write for the Love Inspired and Love Inspired Suspense lines. Lenora also wrote a weekly opinion column for the local paper and worked freelance for years with a local magazine. She has now turned to full-time fiction writing and enjoying adventures with her retired husband, Don. Married for thirty-six years, they have two grown children. Lenora enjoys writing, reading and shopping...especially shoe shopping.

Bayou Sweetheart
Lenora Worth

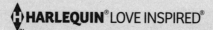 HARLEQUIN® LOVE INSPIRED®

Recycling programs
for this product may
not exist in your area.

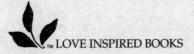

™ LOVE INSPIRED BOOKS

ISBN-13: 978-0-373-81739-9

BAYOU SWEETHEART

Copyright © 2014 by Lenora H. Nazworth

www.Harlequin.com

Printed in U.S.A.

He shall come down like rain upon the mown grass:
as showers that water the earth.
—*Psalms* 72:6

To Margie Clarkston and her sweet son Dennis.
Thank you for reading my books!

Chapter One

A woman danced in the rain in his garden.

Tomas Delacorte stared out the big upstairs window of Fleur House, oblivious to the coming storm. Instead, he watched the graceful woman as she lifted her face to the clouds and laughed, her long ponytail trailing around her shoulder like a flower vine, her hands out, palms up, as if she were saying a prayer. Her colorful tiered skirt was as bright as the various containers of flowers surrounding her. She had kicked off her sandals and now danced with barefoot abandon in the freshly mowed grass that sloped down to the bayou.

This must be Callie Moreau. The landscape lady.

He inhaled a deep breath. A sensation passed through his chest like a fresh wind and stirred up the dust inside his heart, causing it to beat a little faster. Causing it to warm and open and absorb. The change almost hurt—the pain of wanting was overwhelming.

She danced. And he fell in love.

He wanted to go out there and dance with her.

He wanted to be that joyous, that happy…just once in his life. But for him, that would be impossible. For him, love didn't work. Just a silly reaction to an unusual sight.

A clap of thunder brought him out of his daydream.

The woman stopped dancing and gazed up at the sky.

Then she turned and looked at the window where he stood.

And into Tomas's eyes.

Callie dropped her head and hurried to the long covered terrace at the back of the huge mansion, her wet clothes and hair making her shiver. Digging into the big tote bag she'd left on the porch, she found her phone and dialed her sister Alma's number.

"He saw me," she said when Alma answered. She had to catch her breath. She'd hurried too fast.

"Who saw you?"

Callie heard the blur of voices echoing over the line along with the sound of a cash register dinging another dollar. Alma was at the Fleur Café, as usual. And it was lunchtime.

"The man. The owner. Tomas Delacorte."

"So *you* saw him? What does he look like?"

"I only got a glimpse before he disappeared. But…tall, dark, handsome. And dark, intense eyes.

Visions of Heathcliff with a little bit of Mr. Darcy thrown in."

"Heathcliff? As in *Wuthering Heights?* That Heathcliff?"

"Yes. That Heathcliff. I think he's bitter and lonely. He must have loved someone and lost them. Brooding. Yes, definitely brooding."

Alma giggled. "Oh, so you know this from a brief glimpse? Tell me more."

She could picture Alma sinking down on a bar stool, her grin reflecting in the aged mirror that ran the length of the counter. "Yes. I was in the garden and it started raining and…I looked up and there he was, staring at me as if he'd just walked out of the pages of a historical romance novel."

"Were you doing the rain dance thing?"

Callie twirled her wet ponytail. "Uh, maybe. Is that bad?"

"No, no. Not bad at all. I'm sure he enjoyed watching you do that silly dance."

"He was watching. I mean, I *felt* him watching. I saw him at the window." Callie went into panic mode. "What if he fires me?"

Alma laughed. "For dancing in the rain? That's not grounds for firing someone."

"But…I wasn't actually doing my job."

"You can't dig dirt in the rain."

"Mr. Tall, Dark and Brooding might think differently."

Callie turned at the sound of footsteps and saw

the very man she'd been talking about standing there staring at her. Again. "Uh, gotta go."

She put away her phone and wiped a hand across her wet hair. "Hello. I'm Callie."

"And apparently I'm Mr.—what was that?—Tall, Dark and Brooding."

Callie's wet skin chilled with a hot blush. She couldn't speak. So she just stood there.

He stepped closer, giving her the full view. Nice, expensive suit, dark sleek hair that curled over his collar in a rebel way. The bluest of blue eyes with dark brows that slashed across his forehead in a perpetual brooding way. Midnight eyes would be cliché. Ocean maybe, but only the deepest, bluest of oceans. Disturbing blue. Yes, disturbing ocean-blue eyes.

Disturbing blue brooding eyes that stayed on her like a spyglass searching for interlopers. Glinting. He was definitely a glinter.

Callie's blush crept like kudzu over her and through her. "I'm sorry to disturb you. I'm the landscaper. I mean, I'm here to work in the garden, to… redo your yard. Nick Santiago hired me."

"I know who you are," he replied, his voice as rough as aged cypress bark. "I saw you out the window." He kept staring. "And I'm pretty sure you know who I am—my real name I mean."

"You're Tomas Delacorte. Nice to finally meet you."

He nodded but didn't return the acknowledgment. "You're wet."

"I'm so sorry," she repeated, wishing she could turn into rain and just wash away. "I was—"

He put his hands in the pockets of his trousers and frowned. "Dancing. In the rain."

She didn't have anywhere to put her hands. "Uh, yes. It's kind of a thing I have…."

The rain turned into a full-blown storm with lashing sheets of water and wind that made her shiver. Callie put her arms against her midsection to ward off the chill from her wet shirt. Maybe these goose bumps weren't from being wet. Maybe this was because of *him*. He glinted at her without moving.

She turned. "I should just go."

He lifted one hand and motioned her toward him. "Come inside out of the rain."

Not used to being ordered, good looks aside, Callie formed her own frown. "I need to get back to town."

"Not in this storm. Come inside. I insist."

When she stood there, frozen and wondering how to get away, he walked a step closer. "Please. I promise I won't lock you in the dungeon."

"You have a dungeon?"

He laughed—almost. And she fell in love. Almost.

Oh, what a beautiful, chiseled face he had. She imagined what it must look like when he truly laughed. What a lovely smile he'd have. Callie decided he probably didn't smile very often. The glint in his eyes changed to a sparkle for just a brief second. So she took this as a rare gift and enjoyed it.

But…she couldn't be in love with him. She'd keep this instant crush to herself. It was the shock of finally meeting him after weeks of speculations, after weeks of her vivid imagination taking over her brain cells. *Get over that,* she told herself. *You don't know this man. You don't even need to know this man. You are content with your life, and you have Elvis.*

Elvis, her big mutt of a dog, would probably scare this straight-out-of-a-menswear-magazine man right out of Fleur. Maybe not scare, but annoy. This man looked like he could become annoyed very easily. And she, Callie Moreau, was known to be the annoying type—the friendly, always sunny, always positive type. So was her dog. Luckily, she'd left Elvis back at the nursery since she'd planned to come and do a quick inspection and then get back to town. She'd been so excited about finally being able to get her hands on the massive, overgrown garden that surrounded Fleur House.

This might not work out so well, after all.

He motioned to her again then pointed toward the big French doors. "We have a basement, but…I'll have Margie and Eunice make you a cup of tea." He frowned. "Isn't that what women love—a good cup of hot tea?"

"This woman does." She marched toward the open, waiting door. "And I'm starving. Do you have anything to eat?"

* * *

"I have a cook," Tomas said, irritated that she had somehow invaded his private space, even more irritated that he'd let her do it by inviting her inside. "And a maid. I'm sure they can feed you something."

"And they could both be on break and probably watching their favorite soap opera." Callie shook her head and smiled that breathtaking smile. "I don't need any help. I—we—don't live like that around here, *Lord* Delacorte."

The sting of that comment pricked his solid armor. He walked to the door off the kitchen and called out, "Margie? Eunice?" Then he pivoted back to Callie. "You don't approve of me having a cook and a maid?"

"Not my business." She pointed to the big, industrial stove. "This kitchen is amazing. Brenna told me it was lovely, but it goes beyond that. It's so… beautiful. Not as fancy as I expected. A good working kitchen. Every woman's dream."

Tomas had to admit it was refreshing to find such a down-to-earth woman. A woman who brought this kitchen to life. But her iridescence was too bright. So he covered his awe with gruffness. "Do you want some tea or not?"

She gave him an exaggerated frown, then toughened her voice. "Yes, but I can make it myself."

Was she mocking him?

The cook and her sister, the housekeeper, both

bustled into the room. Hired help, but more like family, they looked at Callie, smiled, then turned to him. "Tomas, did you need something?"

Tomas held up his ringing cell phone but answered Margie before he took the call. "Tea and food, for our guest."

"Hi," Callie said, smiling. "I'm Callie and I can make my own tea. Iced or hot, either way is good."

"Nonsense," Eunice replied. The two women started chattering away as they went about serving Callie.

Tomas nodded to Margie and Eunice, then turned and left the room. But he couldn't help but eavesdrop on the feminine introductions and laughter coming from the kitchen. Not used to the echo of such joy, he shut his office door with a bang.

He didn't like the feelings this colorful, full-of-life woman evoked in him. He didn't have time for such feelings. Used to controlling everything and everyone, Tomas got the impression he'd never control Callie Moreau. Besides, he had work to do. Taking over a major company was never easy. Soon he'd be the most hated man in town.

Callie Moreau would hate him, too. And that would be that.

A few minutes later, a knock at his door brought his head up. "Yes?"

The door slowly opened and Eunice stuck her head in. "I've brought lunch and…Callie wanted a word with you."

Before Tomas could protest, Callie was in, holding a lunch tray, and Eunice was gone, the door shut.

Callie's smile looked tentative, but he saw the hint of empathy in her pretty gray-blue eyes. "We had grilled ham and cheese. I brought one for you."

"I don't like grilled ham and cheese."

"Really? I thought everyone loved grilled ham and cheese sandwiches on a rainy day. When was the last time you had one?"

He sat back, memories swirling around him like the mist hitting the big windows. "It's been a long time."

She set down the tray on the edge of his massive desk. "Then this is going to be a good day."

He nodded, turned sarcastic. "In more ways than one, apparently."

She blushed, fussed with his napkin and water glass. "I hope the weather lets up. I have a lot to do. I love the rain, of course. But I want to make your garden a stunner. I need dry earth and sunshine for that."

Tomas prayed for rain all day, then changed his mind and prayed for sunshine. He didn't want her to go, but he certainly didn't want her stay. "You need to talk to me?"

She nodded.

He motioned to a chair.

After she'd settled her skirt and smoothed her hair, she gave him a direct glance, then produced some papers from the tote bag draped over her arm.

"I wanted to show you the grid for the garden. Nick approved everything, but I'd feel better knowing you approve things, too. I'm not used to taking over someone's garden without their input."

He waved that notion away. "Nicholas sings your praises. I trust his judgment."

She flipped her ponytail. "He has to sing my praises. He's going to be my brother-in-law in two weeks." Then she sat up in her chair. "You live here. I'd like your input."

Tomas stared at the sandwich on his plate, the scent of buttered bread making his stomach growl. "If you insist."

"I do. It's how I do business, Mr. Delacorte."

Interesting. Some bite behind all that bright.

"Tomas," he replied. "Call me Tomas."

"Well, Tomas, eat your lunch and then we'll get to work."

What a bossy woman.

"It's still raining. Why don't you call it a day?"

"I don't melt in the rain," Callie replied, a sweet shyness seeming to envelop her.

"No, I have no doubt there. I think you thrive in the rain. At least it looked that way to me earlier."

"I didn't know you were watching."

"I didn't know when I looked out the window I'd find you down there dancing in the rain."

She pushed the plate toward him, determination taking over her chirpiness. "Eating will get rid of that bad mood."

"Who said I'm in a bad mood?"

"So you're like this all the time?"

Tomas thought about that. "Yes, pretty much."

He was rewarded with what looked like a doubtful but challenging smile. Tomas bit into the thick French bread and tasted the rich white cheddar and the salty ham, the spicy-sweet mustard covered with a ripe tomato from the farmer's market in town. Then he glanced over at Callie. "This is by far the best ham and cheese sandwich I've ever eaten."

She giggled. "You need to get out more."

"That's probably true."

If he had this woman to entice him, Tomas might become less of a recluse and more of a social human being.

But, he reminded himself, he had not come back to Fleur, Louisiana, to fling himself into a relationship. He'd come back here to prove something to all the people who'd once scorned him and condemned him. And prove it he would, without distraction.

He dropped the sandwich and pushed the plate away, his appetite gone.

What would the lovely Callie Moreau think when she found out the truth about him? When she found out who he really was?

He didn't want that to happen yet. He could control how much she knew in the same way he controlled everything else in his life.

"Let's get on with this," he said in an abrupt tone. "I have a busy afternoon."

She nodded, shuffled her folded papers and came around the desk. "Here's the grid."

Tomas sniffed the floral scent of her perfume while she expounded on everything from Japanese maples to cast-iron plants.

And he wondered why he even cared about the garden in the first place.

"So that's how Alma's gumbo got so famous."

Callie grinned over at Margie and Eunice. She remembered seeing them at church when they'd come for the first time a few weeks ago, so she felt at ease with them. After lunch, Himself had gone off to take another important call, but the rain kept falling so she was now back in the kitchen. Would she ever get to dig in that garden?

"So what's it like to work for such a scary person?" she asked, killing time with small talk.

"We like him," Margie said. She shot a covert glance to the other end of the big house. "He pays well."

"Okay, that's good. He's generous then?"

"Very," Eunice chimed in. "But we've known Tomas for a long time now. That's why we came to work here. He only asks that we keep things straight and clean. He doesn't mind us taking breaks. And he told us we could take off anytime we had doctor's appointments or things like that." She shrugged. "We hardly know he's around."

"Good." Callie twirled her hair, remembering her

time with Tomas in his office. The man couldn't
wait to get rid of her. "So you're telling me that Mr.
Delacorte isn't really that scary?"

Both women went very quiet. Callie wondered if
they hadn't heard her. "So?"

"Boo."

She turned to find Tomas standing in the door-
way to the kitchen. He'd managed to sneak up on
her yet again and while she was talking about him,
yet again. When had he managed to walk the whole
house without her hearing?

"Oh, hi." She sat still while Margie and Eunice
jumped up and pretended to be doing busy stuff.
"Is that rain still out there?" And when would she
learn to keep her mouth shut?

"Did I scare you?" he asked, ignoring the rain
question.

"No. I mean, yes." It was time for her to go home.

He gave her the glint look. "Voices tend to echo
through this house."

"I'll keep that in mind."

After the other women beat a hasty exit, he leaned
against the counter. "Do I…scare you?"

Callie couldn't fudge the truth. She was known
for her sugar-coated bluntness, after all. "Yes, you
do. You're different."

"In what way?"

*In a tingling, strange way that messes with my
head.*

She lifted her hand, indicating their surroundings,

and thought of the first excuse that came to mind. "This house didn't come cheap."

Fleur House was a true treasure with its many porches and porticos, the arched windows and terraces and that garden, lush with possibilities. This man had bought it, commissioned Nick Santiago to renovate it and had managed to put a big intricate iron fence around it to keep everyone out.

But all of that added up to a lot of money.

"No, but how does that make me different?"

"Have you really taken a look at this town? We're hurting. Between storms, oil spills and a bad economy, we're barely hanging on. But you—you seem to have it all together. You get to live in a beautiful, historic home. You obviously have money since you poured a lot into renovating this place. And you're paying me a hefty fee to spruce up the property. So yes, you're different. You don't have to worry about where your next paycheck will come from."

He leaned close to her, his gaze heating her skin. "I am different, but not in the way you think."

Callie took a breath and dug right in. "You want to explain that?"

"No," he said. Then he glanced out the row of kitchen windows. "Oh, look, the rain's stopped."

Callie knew a dismissal when she heard one.

"My cue to leave," she said. Grabbing her tote and her pride, she turned at the back door. "I'll be back tomorrow. Hopefully, the ground will be dry by then. I'll try to stay out of your way."

"I'd appreciate that—you coming back to finish the job *and* you staying out of my way." He nodded, glinted and then turned and walked out of the room.

Chapter Two

"So you will be at the wedding?"

Tomas walked with Brenna and Nick to their car. They'd come by to take one last look at the house that they'd both helped renovate. Tomas always enjoyed meetings that involved Brenna. She knew her art, and she had fallen in love with his right-hand man, Nicholas Santiago.

He stared at Brenna now. She was different from her sisters. All auburn and fire, lots of emotion and drama. Alma was maternal and earthy, with golden-brown hair and flashing eyes.

And Callie. She was earth, wind and fire, water and sunshine. The total package. Sunlight-golden hair and gray-blue eyes. He hadn't seen her since they'd met the other day, but he'd seen traces of her work in the garden. Would she only come around when he wasn't here?

"Earth to Tomas?" Brenna grinned over at him. "I think we lost you there for a minute. Did you think of something else we need to do for you? For the house?"

"No." Tomas kept smiling. "The wedding? Yes, I plan to be there. Wouldn't miss it." Dreaded it with all his heart, but…he'd promised Nick.

Brenna let out a little squeal. "Good. You know, everyone in town is dying to meet the mysterious man who bought Fleur House. You're a hot topic around here."

Nick shook his head. "Anybody new here is a hot topic. Don't let her tease you."

Tomas enjoyed the way they glanced at each other. So in love. He thought of Callie, dancing in the rain. Remembered he didn't want her dancing in his garden. Remembered her laughing in his kitchen. Remembered that he didn't want her laughing in his kitchen. Or in his garden, for that matter.

"We've lost him again," Brenna said, opening the trunk of her car to put away some folders. "Tomas, please don't disappoint me. I want you to be at my wedding. I owe you a lot, you know. If you hadn't bought this house, I wouldn't have met Nick."

"That's true, *sí,*" Nick said, nodding his agreement. "Say yes, so she'll quit pestering you."

Brenna tilted her head. "My sisters are my bridesmaids. Callie will be wearing a pretty blue dress."

That got his attention. "Ah, Callie. I met her the other day. She was…in the garden."

"She loves that job," Brenna replied, a twinkle in

her eye. "She told Alma and me about how you'd caught her playing in the rain."

He was sure she'd told them more—that he was brooding and scary and that she had a total disdain for his lofty lifestyle.

"She's a very…interesting woman."

Nick grinned and winked. "These Blanchard sisters, Tomas. Have to watch them."

Brenna didn't even bat an eye. "It's Callie Blanchard Moreau now, but she is the last Blanchard woman standing. The strongest of us. You need to ask her to dance at the wedding so she won't feel like a wallflower. Okay?"

"I don't dance," Tomas replied, already imagining Callie in a blue dress, in his arms. Definitely not a wallflower.

Brenna shook her head at that. "You might change your mind." She was about to shut the trunk when Tomas stopped her.

"Wait," he said, spying a painting lying in the trunk underneath a blanket. The blanket had slipped away to reveal long blond hair and one sky-blue eye. "May I see that?"

Brenna pulled at the blanket. "I painted it." She beamed and sent a glance to her amused fiancé. "For Callie's birthday, last December. Papa and I have been working on the frame. Only Callie is a bit embarrassed about it. She didn't want people to think she's vain so she asked Papa to keep it."

Tomas lifted the painting and held it up. It was a

portrait of Callie laughing in a garden. It reminded him of the other day. The day his heart had beat faster. "How much?"

Brenna frowned over at him. "Excuse me?"

"I want to buy this. How much?"

Nick cleared his throat. "Uh, that's not for sale. Brenna gave it to Callie as a gift."

"But she refused to accept it." Tomas held tight to the painting. Brenna had captured her sister's essence, the same essence he'd seen when she was in the garden. "I understand that and I appreciate it. But I'd like to buy this painting."

Brenna started to speak, then stopped, then started again.

"I...I don't know what to say. I mean, I worked on it for months, sometimes right here in the sunroom, before the house was finished. Papa said he'd like to hang it by our mother's portrait."

"How much?" Tomas asked again. "Name your price."

Brenna dropped the blanket into the trunk. "But...what will I tell Callie? And Papa? Have you met my papa?"

"No. But I've met your sister. Just quote me a price."

Brenna walked over to Nick. "Will you please explain to your boss that this portrait is not for sale?"

Nick grinned again. "I think Tomas has finally met his match." He leaned close to Brenna. "And I'm not talking about you and your papa."

Brenna smiled at Nick, a gleam in her eyes. "Tomas, I can't sell you the portrait. But I'm flattered that you like it."

Tomas put the portrait back in the trunk. "I'm sorry. I didn't mean to make demands. It's just that—"

"This would be perfect in one of the bedrooms," Brenna replied, her eyes lighting up.

"I had thought the sunroom." Tomas shouldn't have said anything. He didn't like the feelings Callie seemed to stir. And he did not like the way Brenna's eyes were gleaming now. She obviously thought he'd gone mad, or she'd sensed his hard-to-explain interest in her older sister.

"The sunroom." Brenna's eyes filled with tears. "Perfect."

"I'm sorry," Tomas said again. "I didn't mean to upset you."

"No, no." Brenna ran a finger over the painting. "Callie has been through so much. So much. I wanted to give her something that would make her smile. She was touched and embarrassed. So we compromised and agreed to display it at Papa's house, maybe in her old room. But…you seem to see her as she is. She's the sunshine in all of our lives."

Tomas swallowed, wondered why he'd even suggested having the painting. "You have to give it back to her—to your family."

Brenna took the painting out and ran her hand over the wooden frame. "My papa made this frame and Alma and I helped Julien and him mat it. Callie probably hasn't even missed it."

"You have to keep it. Because you're family," Tomas said again, a trace of regret in the words. "I understand. You all had a part in this gift."

Brenna stared at Callie's image. "Yes. But Callie would be so touched that you wanted it. She needs to know that someone wants—"

"I understand," Tomas finished, feeling awkward now.

Brenna turned to Nick. "What should I do?"

Nick shrugged. He kissed her on the nose. "Remember you and me? Remember?"

"Yes." She took his hand. "We're so blessed."

Tomas could see their love. But he wasn't sure what they were saying. "Obviously, I've upset you."

Nick held out a hand. "The Blanchard sisters lost their mother to breast cancer. They get emotional about things."

"I'm sorry." Tomas wished he'd never suggested buying the painting. He was usually better at handling negotiations. "Put it away, Brenna."

"I don't mind you having it," Brenna said. "I think it's a beautiful idea. But…Callie's been hurt badly by a horrible divorce. Her ex-husband couldn't handle it when she got sick."

Tomas lifted his head and stared at Brenna, his heart hammering as realization hit him like a hot wind. "Callie? She was…sick?"

"She's a cancer survivor," Brenna replied. "But…"

"But you don't want anyone to hurt her ever again," Tomas finished. "I understand. That's a family thing, too."

"Yes. We're close. Tight-knit. I'd have to explain."

And he'd have to promise to honor that gift and the woman he'd met the other day. Callie…with cancer. He didn't like thinking about that. He wasn't sure he was ready for something so strong, so tightly woven.

How could he even begin to understand what Brenna was saying to him? She didn't want him to make a mess of her sister's life. He didn't want to be in anyone's life anyway.

"Take it back to your father."

Brenna wrapped the painting and placed it in the trunk. "Thanks for understanding."

Tomas usually liked a good challenge. But this was a matter of the heart, and it had been a very long time since he'd given his heart to anything that truly mattered. "Don't tell her I asked to buy it."

"Of course not," Brenna replied, her eyes full of hope and understanding. "If this portrait of my sister ever does wind up in your home, you'll have to be the one to tell her. But you need to know—she likes surprises. The good kind, that is."

"Thank you," Tomas said. "It was good to see both of you."

Then he turned and headed toward his big, lonely house.

* * *

"Surprise!"

Callie clapped her hands and beamed with glee. They'd planned a special shower for Brenna, the last one before her wedding, at Alma's little cottage on the bayou.

"What is all of this?" Brenna asked as she moved through the dainty living room. "I already have so much from my other showers."

"We know," Alma said, smiling. "This is from us—your sisters and your close friends."

Callie pulled Brenna close. "See—Winnie's here and Pretty Mollie and—"

"And the other waitresses from the café and Mrs. LeBlanc and Mrs. Laborde," Brenna finished. "So thoughtful. What do you two have up your sleeve?"

"Wait until you see your gifts," Callie said, her heart bursting. After going through a bad breakup and losing her dream job in Baton Rouge, Brenna had found Nick—a wonderful man—to spend her life with, a man who recognized her talents and her temperamental, creative nature. Callie's heart pierced at the thought of her sisters finding happiness. She'd thought she had it. Once. Long ago. But Dewayne Moreau was nowhere to be seen in Louisiana. He was long gone.

But she was here. She'd survived a divorce and breast cancer. Now she was grateful for each breath she took. Her prayers were sweeter, deeper, with more meaning. Because she'd been given a true second chance. Every minute had to count.

She missed their mother, Lola. "Mom would be so happy for you," she told Brenna.

"I know. I know." Brenna went around, looking at the presents scattered here and there. "What kind of shower is this, anyway?"

Callie and Alma both laughed. "It's an artist type shower. Your husband-to-be has big plans for that new house he's building you."

Brenna's expression went soft. "He's so sweet. I can't believe he decided we could live here part-time."

"He loves you. And…you will be going back and forth between here and San Antonio," Callie said.

"And he does have that adorable little hacienda in Texas," Alma reminded her sister. "You are blessed."

Brenna's eyes grew bright. "But really, what kind of shower is this?"

"Oh, all right, impatient," Callie retorted. "We bought you art supplies for that new studio Nick's including in your house."

Brenna burst into tears.

"Drama queen," Callie said, grabbing her little sister close. "Why are you crying?"

"I…I just never dreamed I'd be so happy," Brenna said through gulps. "I…I want all of us to be this happy." She looked at Callie. "I want you—"

"Shh," Callie said, her own tears hot against her

cheek. "I'm always happy. Always. I get to see both of you married to good men. I get to design the garden of my dreams at Fleur House. I have Elvis. He's the perfect companion."

Out on the porch, Elvis barked in agreement.

Brenna's tears disappeared. "What do you think of Tomas? Isn't he so…mysterious?"

And so the conversation turned to the man who'd been centered in Callie's mind for over two weeks. She'd been out to the house a couple more times, but he'd been away on business or off doing whatever a mysterious man did. Or maybe he'd been there, but he'd studied her from that lofty view up above the tree line, where people who didn't want to be seen lived. Maybe he was some sort of superhero who fought crime by night and built empires by day.

"So…?"

She looked up to find several big-eyed women staring at her. "Oh, the punch. Yes, it's almost ready."

"We weren't talking about punch," Alma retorted with a wry grin. "Have you been doing any more dancing?"

"Oh, hush." Callie busied herself with getting ice and mixing the creamy concoction of standard shower punch.

Winnie raised her hand. "I hear he reminds you of Heathcliff."

Pretty Mollie, one of the younger waitresses at

the Fleur Café located in front of Alma's cottage, giggled. "Heathcliff, as in *Wuthering Heights?*"

"That Heathcliff, yes," Alma replied. Mollie dated her husband, Julien's, younger brother, Pierre.

"Can't you ever keep the things I tell you to yourself?" Callie asked, blood rushing to her cheeks.

"It's payback time," Brenna said, still sniffing. "You've been teasing us about men for years now. It's our turn."

"But that was about men you were involved with," Callie said. She stirred the lime sherbet into the lemon-lime fizzing soda with a vengeance, then added some fruit juice. "This is different."

"Is it really?" Brenna asked. "He seems keen on you."

"What makes you think that?" Callie asked, her heart pounding just as much as the wooden spoon she used to attack the sherbet. She wasn't sure what "keen on you" actually meant.

Brenna put a hand over her mouth. "Oh, nothing. He just mentioned how he'd met you and that you were…interesting."

Pretty Mollie put on a dreamy smile. "Isn't it romantic? A handsome stranger who lives in a big old house all by himself. What's his story anyway?"

A sigh moved through the roomful of women.

Brenna glanced from Alma to Callie. "I've heard things."

"What things?" Callie asked. Brenna remained silent. "What things, Brenna?"

"Nick told me not to tell."

"You can't just throw that out there and expect us to accept that," Callie replied, worry clouding over her annoyance at her sister's teasing. "Is there something I should know about the man?"

Brenna studied the faces in the room, drawing out the anticipation until Callie thought she'd scream. "Brenna?"

Brenna shook her head. "I don't know if it's true but...I think he was married before."

"And?" Callie closed her eyes, the answer already forming in her brain.

"And she died. Mysteriously."

"Of course," Callie replied, hope melting into a puddle right along with the sherbet. She'd figured divorced. But this was tragic, just like the man. It explained a lot, however.

"Define *mysteriously,*" Alma said.

"No one knows what happened," Brenna replied. "He took her away and then he came back to Texas without her. He doesn't talk about it." She turned stern, her gaze sweeping the room. "And we can't talk about it. We all know how closemouthed men can be."

"No wonder," Mrs. Laborde, who loved to pass on tall tales, said on a low whisper. "Callie, be careful when you go out there."

Callie stood up straight. "This is ridiculous. Brenna, remember we wondered what the deal was with Nick? Now we know he lost a family member.

That's why he was so standoffish and mysterious. It could be the same with Tomas. He loved his wife and he tried to save her."

"Maybe," Alma said. "Or maybe…"

Callie held up a hand. "Maybe he couldn't handle things and he bolted. I know all about that, don't I?"

She looked at her sisters, saw the sympathy and the fear in their eyes. "I'm working for the man. That's all. I'll be okay."

But she had to wonder, as she poured punch into pretty blue cups, if she'd made a fatal mistake in accepting this job.

Not if you keep to yourself and guard your heart, she thought. *Not if you stay busy doing what you were hired to do and never enter that beautiful house again.*

She wouldn't think about Tomas Delacorte as a lonely, brooding man who might need a friend. She wouldn't.

But of course, she was just the kind of person who befriended everyone anyway. Even if they didn't want her around.

Chapter Three

"So the sale is final and all the paperwork is in place. We can finally announce our plans to the public."

Nick sat across from Tomas's antique walnut desk, taking notes on his tablet. "Good. Do you want to see the preliminary plans for the updated factory? The main office blueprints are included."

Tomas took the rolled-up blueprints and spread them out on the desk. "They're finished?"

"As of last night. I had to get them done or risk upsetting my bride. She decided she does want to go on a honeymoon, after all. We're still trying to decide where however, since we've both been so busy we've held off until the last minute."

Tomas smiled at that. "Brenna is a forceful female."

"And don't I know it," Nick replied, his eyes bright with contentment. "She amazes me."

Tomas swallowed his envy and let the lump settle in his stomach. He'd given up on the love thing long ago. "You're blessed." He reached inside the desk drawer and pulled out an envelope. "I want to go ahead and give you this now. In case your forceful bride doesn't approve of my gift."

"What's this?" Nick took the big envelope and opened it. After skimming the contents, he looked up at Tomas. "A trip to Paris? Are you kidding me?"

"I hope not," Tomas replied. "You can schedule it, but your honeymoon is on me."

"I...I don't know what to say." Nick stared down at the itinerary. "Brenna had hoped we'd get to do this one day. But for our honeymoon, we'd thought a quick trip to Florida or maybe California. But Paris... She'll be thrilled."

Tomas enjoyed seeing the glee in his friend's dark eyes. "I know it seems extravagant, but I pretty much depended on both of you, and your aunt Serena, too, to put this house together for me. You did a great job and then you went right into renovating plans for the other property. This is my way of thanking you."

"What did you give my aunt?" Nick quipped.

"Serena, well, she's hard to please. She only wanted to bid on my next project. She'll be decorating the offices at the business property here, for starters."

"Oh, she'll like that," Nick said, grinning. "You know, she and Brenna's father have a thing."

"A thing? As in, a relationship thing?"

"Sí." Nick shook his head. "It was awkward at first, but Brenna and I have accepted it. They're good for each other and they both agree it's for companionship—for now."

Tomas stood and turned to stare out the ceiling-to-floor window behind his desk. He could see part of the bayou from this viewpoint. Banana fronds and palmetto palms waved back at him as they danced in the spring breeze. A snowy white egret standing down in the shallows lifted her head in a pose. "This place seems to bring out the romantic in everyone."

"You, too?" Nick asked, getting up to gather his papers.

Tomas turned around. "You know I'm not wired that way."

"You might change that tune." Nick came around the desk and shook Tomas's hand. "Thank you, Tomas. For the trip. Brenna will be beside herself."

"I want you to enjoy being newlyweds," Tomas replied. "I mean that."

"We will. See you later." Nick turned and headed out of the room.

Tomas pivoted back to the window and saw a flash of something big and gangly moving through the backyard.

What kind of beast was that?

He shifted to see around the corner. There it was again.

A horse? No, a dog. A big, splotchy black-and-white dog that had paws the size of a Clydesdale's hooves. The animal starting barking, then took off to chase a hapless squirrel. The squirrel rushed up the nearest live oak while the dog stood waiting and woofing.

Then Tomas heard a feminine voice calling. "Elvis, hush up. We don't want to disturb Himself."

"Himself?" Tomas actually chuckled. "Is that what she calls me now?"

He tried hard to frown, but his mood immediately lightened and his feet moved without any logic toward the nearest door to the outside.

Callie was back in *his* garden. And apparently she'd brought her guard dog with her. He'd have to insist that she put that animal away. He silently practiced what would be a stern lecture as he hurried toward the sunny backyard.

Callie laughed at Elvis, thinking he should have figured out by now that squirrels always got away. The big dog turned and stared at her, as if to say "Hey, a little help here."

"C'mon over here," she said, slapping a hand against her jeans. "We've got work to do."

Elvis looked offended by that statement, but he finally gave a grudging, low bark and galloped back toward her. When he was about a foot away, however, he skidded to a stop, his big brown eyes moving beyond Callie.

"What do you see now?" she asked, turning.

Tomas Delacorte stood on the back terrace, staring down at them with that lord-of-the-manor frown.

"Hello." Callie waved and Elvis took that as his cue to head on up and greet the interloper.

Callie stood up to stop the meeting of dog and man, but she was too late. "Elvis, no!"

Elvis barked with glee and went right on up the terrace steps and lifted up for a paw-hug. Tomas stepped back, his frown increasing, his hands up in the air. Elvis lifted, grabbed hold, pawed and left mud stains on Tomas's expensive-looking gray suit.

"Elvis, get down," Callie called as she rushed up toward the house. This wouldn't be pretty. Tomas would probably tell her he hated dogs. Elvis would be banished from ever coming here again. And… so would she.

By the time she'd made it to the terrace, breathless and winded and wondering why she'd brought the dog in the first place, Tomas had Elvis by his collar.

"What is this?" he asked, his eyes flashing anger.

"My dog," she said, her tone defensive. "Let him go."

Tomas held Elvis at arm's length. "Get him out of my yard."

"He goes where I go," she replied. "For protection."

Tomas dropped his hand. Elvis immediately leaped back up against him. "He doesn't exactly act like a guard dog."

"He…alerts me," she replied on a weak note.

This man made her so nervous. She wasn't used to dealing with such a dour, unpleasant person.

Tomas gave her a pointed look and held Elvis by his paws so he could push the big dog off of his suit.

"Elvis, down," Callie said, grabbing the dog to tug him away. "I'm sorry. Once he gets used to you, he won't do that."

"I don't want him to get used to me. I want him away."

Callie shooed Elvis out into the yard and dug in her heels for a fight. "Listen, this dog goes where I go. Sometimes I'm out in a garden alone until almost dark. He at least barks and lets me know when someone is approaching."

Tomas brushed at his ruined suit. "And attacks."

"I'll have that cleaned for you."

"No need. Just…keep him off the porch."

"He usually sleeps or chases squirrels."

"Fine."

She took a breath. "We're not sure what breed— or breeds—he is. He showed up at the nursery one day and wouldn't leave. So he's mine now."

Tomas shot her a look that encompassed the meaning of that phrase. "You take in strays?"

"Not normally. Only the really good-looking ones."

He gave her another look, surprise on his face. Did he consider himself a stray? Did he consider letting her take him in?

"You named him Elvis?"

"Yeah, 'cause he's a hunk, a hunk of burnin' love."

Tomas didn't laugh, but she saw that sparkle in the dark blue of his eyes. Okay, now they were getting down to business. She'd been reprimanded and Elvis had been banished.

Yet she had to defend her dog. "I like his company. He's playful, watchful and he doesn't ask a lot of questions."

His eyebrows quirked upward. "*You* don't like questions?"

"Who does?"

Tomas walked down to where she stood on the bottom step. Elvis hurried back then sniffed and took off after something that moved. Probably the wind.

Tomas surprised her by sitting back on the terrace edge. Shocked yet again, Callie thought she should tell him she had work to do. She should call her dog and leave. She should be aloof and unattainable, mysterious and standoffish.

But no, here she stood waiting for his next words. Pathetic, really. "Did you need something else?" she asked, as if she really meant it. "I did come here to work."

He stared off into the distance. "I don't get out in the garden much."

"You work a lot. It's understandable. And speaking of that, what exactly do you do?"

He loosened his tie then put his hands between his knees and stared out toward the bayou. "I buy things."

"I can see that," she said, lifting her hand toward the house. "You buy big expensive things."

"Yes. Buildings, companies, factories, mostly commercial real estate."

"People? Do you try to buy people?"

His frown turned stoic, but she saw a trace of tenderness in his eyes. "I've found most people can't be bought."

"But you've tried?"

"Are you asking me this because you're curious, or because you think I'm that kind of man?"

"Maybe both."

"What would you like to know about me, Callie?"

She had to be her usual blunt self. "Everything. Nothing. It's not my business, after all."

"But you've heard things? You want to know why I'm here."

"We'd all like to know that."

She wanted to shout that she needed to know about his wife. About what had happened with his wife. Did he love her? Or did he abandon her? Was she still alive and hiding in some attic somewhere far away?

Her gaze drifted up to the oval second-story balcony. Maybe he'd brought his wife here.

He got up. "I'm holding a meeting with the city

council on Thursday. Of course, the public is welcome to come."

"Are you inviting me?"

"Are you a member of the public?"

"Yes."

"Then you're welcome to come."

Talking to this man was not easy. He held everything in with a perpetual frown. He seemed practiced and practical, as if he didn't dare cut loose like a normal human being. She wondered did he ever show any emotion, ever lose his temper. Ever hurt.

She turned too quickly and almost stumbled. Right into him. He took her by the arm and helped her, his touch fleeting and swift and then gone. But the warm imprint lingered white-hot against her skin, teasing at her senses like the playful wind.

"Can you give me a hint now?" she asked to distract herself from that brief touch.

He stared at her arm then looked at his hand. "Industry. That's your hint."

"Industry. Hmm. Does this mean jobs? We'd heard rumors about the shipyard."

"Possibly."

His gaze swept over her as if he expected her to dispute his words. Callie didn't know what to say. They heard rumblings about things around here on a daily basis. They'd find out the truth, good or bad, soon enough.

And yet, she couldn't resist asking. "Are you here to do something about those rumors?"

"I have to go and change into a clean suit," he said. Then he turned and went inside the house.

Callie went back to her work, wondering if Tomas Delacorte was in Fleur to bring about more jobs or if he had come to take over a struggling company. Was he here for good or for evil?

She couldn't decide. Her heart told her he was a good man. He'd been great about giving Brenna free rein on finding art pieces to display in his big remodeled Italianate-style mansion. Nick sang his praises even when he hadn't been allowed to tell them who his boss was.

Now that she'd met him, Callie tried to see the goodness in Tomas. He hadn't actually banned Elvis from his property. That gained him points. If Elvis liked the man, that was good enough for her.

But she sensed a dark sadness in him, too. His rare, forced smiles held a trace of tragedy, of loss.

Did he mourn his *allegedly* dead wife? Or was he bitter about losing her? Did he leave her the way Dewayne had left Callie, because he couldn't handle illness and death? Did he have a secret?

Shaking her head, Callie decided not to go down that path. Instead, she focused on the row of daylilies she was planting in a sunny spot in the side garden. She'd have more people to help her next week, but for now she wanted to enjoy being alone and creating new paths in this old, settled garden. During the earlier scouting expeditions she'd taken out here, she'd found a wealth of aged shrubs and bushes. Azaleas hidden underneath weeds and bramble, old camellia bushes and crape myrtles hiding behind pine shrubs and palmetto plants, and climbing roses tossed in with hydrangeas underneath tallow trees and piles of brittle pine straw.

A treasure trove of possibilities. A gardener's dream.

She patted down the rich soil around the final daylily plant, her intention to have these tender shoots nurtured into blooms by the end of spring.

Brenna was trying to talk Tomas into holding an open house and a spring picnic, so Callie wanted the gardens to be in good shape for that. These lilies would come back each spring and grow and multiply if she had her way. She'd talked to them and suggested they behave and show off a bit now that they had found a good home.

Having finished up, she turned toward the sun that moved gently into dusk over the bayou. Then she looked back at the big house looming like a lost castle behind her.

Once, long ago, she'd dreamed of living in this mansion. It had been a true daydream, a little girl's fantasy of being the lady of Fleur House. Now, while the house looked all fresh and prim and glowing, she wondered about the sadness that seemed to shroud it. Or rather the sadness that seemed to wear like a mantle on the owner's broad shoulders.

"I can't get involved in any sadness," she stated

to herself in a whisper that followed the wind. "I'm happy now. Free. Content. Sadness is not allowed."

But were dreams allowed?

She brushed her dirty hands down the side of her old work jeans and stretched like a contented cat. She'd had a good day, interruptions by Himself aside. This particular bed, centered between the bayou and the back terrace, was ready for show. She'd positioned a Japanese maple in the middle and had spread out from there with the lilies and some other bulbs. This garden should have something to brag about for most of the year, even some playful spider lilies here and there.

Would he approve?

She turned to gather her work tools. There was a spigot on the side of the house by the terrace. She'd wash her things and her hands there. The buzz of mosquitoes teased at her ears as she made her way up the sloping hills toward the house, Elvis now meandering in an end-of-day tiredness behind her. Last fall, a hurricane had washed through Fleur, knocking everything in this garden over in rushing waters and driving winds.

But it was spring now. A new season with tender surprise sprouts that promised their own kind of mystery. That promised a determined survival and rebirth.

"Just like me," she said, smiling. She silently thanked God for the beauty of this moment.

She'd made it to the spigot and was busy cleaning her tools when the back door opened and *he* walked out.

"All finished?" he asked.

Callie bent and turned off the spigot. "Yes. I'm tired but pleased. One flower bed down, about a hundred or so to go."

"You're going to bring in help, right?"

"Yes." She noticed he'd changed into jeans and a cotton button-down shirt. The casual outfit only added to his good looks. And made him seem relaxed, just like a normal person. "Yes, I'll have lots of help."

"Hire as many people as you need."

Noting this new, mellow mood, she said, "You're very generous."

"I've never had a big garden like this before. I want it to be appropriate to the house."

She told herself to say goodbye and go home. But she turned after making sure she had all her tools. "Where did you grow up?"

He stared off into the distance, that darkness shrouding him like the sky lifting to the full moon. "Not far from here."

He looked from the horizon to her, a dare in his expression.

"Really? Maybe I know the town."

"You don't." Then he did that turning-and-walking-away thing again.

Which made Callie want to stomp her feet. She prided herself on being a people person. She wasn't used to being treated this way. "Hey," she called, hoping to open a dialogue, "why do you do that?"

"Do what?"

"Just walk back into the house. Don't you want to see what I've done with the gardens so far?"

"I know what you've done," he replied, his back to her.

"How do you know?"

"I watch you sometimes."

"I'm not so sure I like being watched. Why don't you just come out and join me? Get involved? You could use some sunshine and fresh air."

He whirled and stalked closer, stared at her, the look in his eyes going dark then changing, going soft. Before she knew what he was doing, he reached up and pushed her long bangs out of her eyes. Callie's breath caught at the gentleness in his touch. It went against the grain of his hardened features.

"You have mud on your forehead," he said, the words as soft as the night wind.

He pulled out a white handkerchief and started wiping at her brow. Callie grabbed his hand and their eyes met, and like a candle flaring in the night, something ignited between them.

"I can do that myself," she said, too shocked to move.

"I know you can," he replied, his gaze sweeping over her face. He held the handkerchief away then stroked it across her brow again, the crisp rasp of cotton scraping over her skin. "There." He gave her the handkerchief then backed away, his eyes still holding hers. "I have to go."

He turned and hurried back into the house.

And left Callie there, spellbound, as she stood caught between the lazy descending sun and the eager rising moon.

Chapter Four

"He grew up near here."

That night at dinner, Callie recounted her talk with Tomas there on the terrace, but she left out the part about him wiping her brow and leaving his monogrammed handkerchief with her. And she left out the part about her washing the silky soft square with a gentle cleanser, her thoughts torn between returning it pressed and folded or keeping it, safe and folded away. Her whole family stared at her as if she were telling a horror story around the camp-fire. Except they were all out on the screened-in back porch of her papa's house and it was a per-fectly pleasant spring evening.

"Nick never mentioned that," Brenna said, a crispy hush puppy making its way to her mouth. "But then, he doesn't ask a lot of questions regard-ing Tomas, and he doesn't gossip about his boss. It's a company rule, so I shouldn't have repeated what he'd already told me about Tomas having a wife who died."

Papa frowned then scratched at his beard stubble. "Dat right dere sounds mighty suspicious to me."

Callie felt his dark, knowing eyes on her. "He's a decent person, Papa. He just likes his privacy. A lot."

Brenna nodded in agreement as she chewed on the hush puppy. "That's true. We have to respect that, whether we like it or not. Which we don't."

"I don't like it, not me," Papa said. He grabbed his glass of sweet tea and took a long sip. "Dere's some talk around the marina about Mr. Delacorte. He's bought up more than a house around here. Word is out that he bought the old shipyard. I hear he might shut the whole thing down. The town council will announce it this week, is what I heard. He's up to something."

Callie's heart bumped against her ribs like a crab caught in a mesh trap. "Something such as?"

"Industry," Brenna replied, clearly keeping *some* secrets for her soon-to-be husband, Nick, since Nick had to work late and wasn't here to speak for himself.

"He mentioned that," Callie replied, bobbing her head, her grilled tilapia growing cold on her plate. "Industry. That's good, though, isn't it?"

Alma glanced over at her husband. Julien looked from her to Callie. "It could be or it might not be, since we've heard he's here to take over the shipyard and give people their walking papers."

"Could he do that?" Callie didn't want to see Tomas in such a light, but maybe she needed to see the truth. He wasn't a hero from a romance novel. He was a real man with a real past and an obvious need to make money. A ruthless, secretive man. And yet, she felt obligated to defend him. "He wouldn't do that."

Papa shook his head. "De shipyard's been in trouble for years now. De Dubois family still holds shares in it, but dey left it adrift long ago. Pierre's hours have been cut. Julien had to give it up years ago and go back to fishing and hunting and taking odd jobs. We all have depended on Fleur Shipyard for a long time now, but times have changed."

"We're doing okay, Papa," Alma said, smiling over at Julien. "Julien's got orders for boats straight through till fall."

"And Nick and Tomas are to thank for that," Brenna said. "They've passed Julien's name around enough to give him extra business. Julien, you might bring old-fashioned boat building back into fashion."

"I can't complain," Julien replied, winking at his wife. Alma elbowed him and smiled. "We're blessed."

Callie picked up on their sly smiles and gentle touches. They sure were glowing for some reason. She supposed being married only a few months did that to people. She couldn't remember glancing at Dewayne in that way, though. Maybe because Dewayne was never pleased with her, no matter how hard she tried to be a good wife.

You're free from all of that, she reminded herself. Callie wasn't the kind to give up, but she never wanted to be married again if it meant she couldn't be the person God had made her to be. If she couldn't dig in the garden or dance in the rain or sing at church or tease her sisters or eat pie just because she loved it, if she couldn't feel free and clear and covered in the love of Christ, she didn't want to be married. Ever. Again.

So being infatuated with a brooding, uptight, closemouthed man wasn't such a hot idea right now.

But Tomas Delacorte did present such an interesting challenge. She liked it when people smiled. Liked being in a happy environment. She wanted to make Tomas smile. That would be her downfall if she wasn't careful.

"We're all blessed," Papa said, bringing Callie back to the real world. "Dat's all fine and dandy." He pushed away from the table and started taking dishes inside to the kitchen through the open French doors. "I just wonder what the man's up to, is all. Why all the hush, hush. I'm sure gonna be at dat council meeting dis week, I can tell you."

"We'll all be there," Callie retorted, caught between loyalty to her town and a need to protect the man who'd offered her a lot of money to redesign his estate grounds. But she'd never been overly impressed with money, except for survival purposes. These feelings had to do with something more, as if God were nudging her to stand by Tomas. "We can hear the truth there." She turned to Brenna. "Nick will be there, right?"

"Yes." Brenna got up and followed their papa. "He's involved in remodeling and renovating any properties Tomas might acquire, so he'll be there. He has to be there."

Was Brenna trying to protect her fiancé? Callie had a lot of questions. They all did. But in her heart, she believed Tomas couldn't be as ruthless and uncaring as her papa might think. He'd thought the same about Julien and Nick, too. Papa just wanted to protect his daughters. And especially her, since he'd never approved of Dewayne. Of course, her ex-husband had never liked her papa very much, either. They'd often argued about her tight-knit family interfering in their lives.

But Papa had been right about Dewayne, she reminded herself. After Papa and Julien headed to the big den across from the kitchen and dining room to watch the evening news, Callie helped her sisters finish cleaning the kitchen.

Through the open screened window, the night sang a lullaby to her. Frogs croaked in a shrill chorus, a mourning dove cooed in a lonely response, a splash sounded in the water and somewhere high in the ancient live oaks, squirrels chased each other.

Callie identified with each of these sounds, these reminders of God's amazing world. The outside world. Her world.

She stood at the sink, staring out at the black waters running down beyond the house, her mind on the man who'd come into her life and now had a spot in her thoughts. Maybe even a spot in her heart. But she had plenty of room in there.

Alma came over to stand by her. "Don't worry. We'll figure this out."

"What's to figure out?" Callie replied. "I'm doing yard work for a strange man. That's what I need to remember. The rest doesn't concern me unless it affects all of us."

Alma gave her a thoughtful glance. "But…you're obviously smitten with Tomas, aren't you?"

Callie laughed. "I'm smitten with the idea of a mysterious man coming to Fleur and moving into the house I've loved all of my life. I'm smitten with the chance to redo those gardens around that house, just the way I've dreamed of doing for most of my life. Beyond that, I can see reality. And we both know reality is a lot harder to do than a fairy tale."

Alma held a hand on Callie's arm, silent for a minute. Then Brenna walked up and put a hand on her other arm. "We want you to be happy again," Alma said, her tone low and sure. "That doesn't mean you have to settle for a man who's handsome, rich, mysterious and single. Not at all."

"Yes." Brenna leaned up and gave Callie a quick kiss. "I mean no. No, not at all."

Callie smiled at their pointed teasing. "I am happy," she replied. "I have no complaints. I'm alive. I get a second chance. Life is good." She gently nudged her sisters away. "Don't feel sorry for me, and don't try to force me onto Tomas Delacorte. I'm thankful. So thankful that I'm living and breathing."

"We are glad for that," Alma said. "So glad."

Her sisters stared at her then glanced at each other. While Callie stood there, ashamed that she hadn't been completely honest with them, and wondered what it would be like to finally be content and happy and in love one more time. She'd survived cancer and was close to her five-year anniversary. She thanked God every day for that.

But she mourned every day for the loss of her marriage. She'd missed a chance to be a mother, to have a family.

Did she deserve a second chance at love?

Tomas and Nick entered the small town hall that stood across from the First Church of Fleur, both wearing lightweight suits and both carrying cell phones and briefcases.

Brenna squealed and hurried to greet Nick.

While Callie stood and stared at Tomas.

The man sure knew how to wear a suit.

Just another reason she should not be so into him.

She was more of a jeans and cotton shirt kind of girl.

Remembering when he'd been wearing jeans and a cotton shirt the other day, Callie swallowed back her intense interest and said a quick prayer against temptation. She'd managed to avoid him for the past couple of days.

Or maybe he'd decided to avoid her.

Until now.

He was walking straight toward her.

"Punch?" she asked, shoving a cup of the lemony mixture into his hand.

"Thanks." He smiled, sipped, studied her in a way that put her on alert. "You have freckles."

"Do I?" She made a big production of rubbing her nose. "Are they gone now?"

His frown almost moved. "No. But they're even brighter now."

Callie wanted to turn and walk away but she had manners, so she stayed and smiled. "I've had them all my life."

"They suit you."

She pushed at her hair and prayed one of her ever-talking sisters would come along and rescue her. But they'd both mysteriously disappeared. "Uh, I had to order some more mulch for the west garden. I'm planting roses there. You do like roses, right?"

He put down the cup of punch. "No roses."

Callie's mouth was still hanging open after he'd walked away.

"What?" Alma hurried up, glancing around as if she expected a fire.

"He doesn't like roses."

"Oh." Alma turned toward where a crowd was gathering for the council meeting. "Is that a deal breaker?"

Callie felt so deflated, she had to remember to breathe. "No, but…it is sad. Who doesn't like roses?"

"They can be overrated," Alma pointed out. "I love yellow ones, though."

"But you love irises more."

Her sister got all dreamy. Probably remembering how Julien had wooed her with blue irises. "That's true."

"It's his wife," Callie replied, her heart hurting with something she couldn't quite identify. "She must have had lots of roses. And she'd walk through her garden every afternoon at sunset, and then she got so sick he had to carry her—"

"Ladies?"

Alma and Callie whirled to find Julien standing there. "What?" Alma asked, smiling at her husband.

"It's about time for the meeting, and I was just wondering if y'all are in charge, or do you want to find a seat?"

"We're coming," Alma replied. She poured him a cup of punch. Then she pushed him ahead of them. "C'mon, Callie. We'll get to the bottom of the rose conspiracy later. Right now, I want to hear what your Mr. Heathcliff is going to say about his real reason for coming to Fleur."

"So do I," Callie replied. She followed her sister to where Brenna was sitting with Pretty Mollie and Julien's brother Pierre. Nick was up front with Tomas, waiting to go before the council. They were first on the agenda. Actually, they were the only item on the agenda tonight. This town council was relaxed and friendly until it came to issues. Then things sometimes got a little heated.

Callie felt that heat each time Tomas glanced back at her. Who didn't like roses?

He didn't. She'd have to find some other flowers to plant in that great big bed she'd worked on for two solid days. She'd show Tomas that she could create a pretty flower garden without roses. She had thousands of other choices anyway.

The councilmen and one woman, Mrs. Laborde, all gathered and sat down. The meeting was called to order and while everyone listened to the clerk go over old business, Callie watched the man who was about to address the entire town.

Tomas Delacorte commanded a presence that left her breathless and confused and wondering and worrying.

And she didn't want to be worried or wondering or out of breath. She didn't want to feel this way about a man who didn't like to smile, about a man who stared out the window instead of coming out into the sunshine. What could she do? What was

there to do, except her job? She'd do her job and
she'd get on with her life and she'd let him do the
same. That was for the best.

But when he stood and walked toward the speaker
podium, she sat up and took notice. And sighed.
Come to think of it, she really didn't like roses all
that much, either.

Tomas had prepared for this moment for months
now. It was never easy buying out a company and
bringing in new people to take over, or possibly
shutting the whole thing down. But he'd thought
long and hard about this because he never made a
move without having a good reason.

What's your reason now? The voice in his head
echoed through his pulse.

He'd come here to show the good people of Fleur
that he was somebody now. That he had power over
them. That he had finally come home to settle an
old score. He had lived near here, very near here.
Just outside town.

But the man he'd hated for most of his life was not
even here to see this day. He wondered as he shuffled
papers and shifted on his butter-soft Italian-made
shoes if any of these people would even remember
or care about a scraggly little boy who stayed hungry and was never really warm.

Then he thought of Callie. She'd care. She'd probably gasp and get up and leave the room. She'd

probably refuse to finish designing his garden and grounds. He thought of her, dancing in the rain.

But he'd come here for a reason so he squared his shoulders and asked God to help him through this. Did God listen to the prayers of a person who'd never bothered to enter a church, a man who'd once been a scared little boy, thrown away and ignored? Could Christ see inside his soul? Would he ever find any peace? Or would he still feel like that lost little boy even after he'd finally gotten his revenge?

Chapter Five

"He's closing down Fleur Shipyard."

"No, he's gonna rebuild it or merge it or something like that. You heard the man."

"What I heard is I'll be let go."

Callie listened to the whispers of conversations going on around her, but she couldn't move, couldn't speak. Tomas Delacorte had come here with a purpose, all right. But she hadn't quite decided if his intentions were good or bad.

Or maybe a little of both. In a voice as smooth as French roast coffee and as commanding as a sea captain, he'd announced that the Fleur Shipyard would be shut down indefinitely in one month. Then after the chaos had finally turned to shocked disbelief, he'd also announced that he would merge the Fleur Shipyard with two others he'd recently acquired, to form Delacorte Shipbuilding and Repair, LLC. This would become a full-service industry with new state-of-the-art technology and the ability to build supply vessels and research vessels and to obtain naval contracts, all backed by a vessel repair service that would be the best in the country. This would be good for the state of Louisiana and especially for Fleur and several other small towns along the Gulf.

That was the press-release, polished version.

Callie wanted the truth, from him.

Brenna poked Callie in the ribs. "What do you think?"

Alma had hopped up to talk to Julien, but Brenna remained beside Callie. Callie glanced around. "I don't know what to think. Papa's not smiling."

"Papa rarely smiles."

"Tomas is not smiling, either."

"He never smiles."

But Callie had seen him smile, kind of. Now he simply sat back and let the discussion continue until it had reached fever pitch. The meeting was over now, after several shouted questions, after mass panic, after reassurances by both Nick and Tomas and after each council member had given it either a blessing or a nay.

"He could have given us this information in a more gradual way," Alma said as she sank back down beside Callie. "I think the old shipyard could use some improvements but I don't know. Steel. This is all about steel. I guess it's a good thing."

"And industry," Callie finally said. "He's bringing new industry to our area. He did tell me that, in a word."

"Only no one wants things to change," Alma replied. "We want the old shipyard. The workers want that one to stay open and running even if it's on its last legs."

"They should want this," Brenna retorted. "A new shipyard is a big change, and if what Tomas told us is true, it could mean jobs, lots of jobs."

"But he also said he might have to let a lot of workers go before he can put his plan into motion," Alma replied. "What will happen to them?"

Brenna lowered her voice. "Some of them are near retirement anyway. He's going to buy them out. He's going to bring in more qualified, more educated, skilled craftsmen. Or at least that's what he just told us."

"Did you know all of this?" Callie asked Brenna.

"No." Her sister shifted on her chair. "I knew he was coming here to do a buyout, but Nick had to be careful about what he said. He's not actually involved in the buyout. He's only involved in building and renovating offices. He'll hire locals for that, at least."

"I've got a bad feeling," Alma said. "A very bad feeling."

Callie didn't know what to say. Did Tomas Delacorte have good intentions? Or was there some other motive for his actions? How long would he leave this town hanging on his promises?

"Surely he has some heavy-duty investors," she said. "I mean, shipyards don't come cheap. You can't just roll into town and say 'I'd like one shipyard, please.'"

"Or two or three." Brenna nodded. "He has investors, yes. Big-shot investors. But he's also a very wealthy man."

"How did he get that way?"

"I'm not sure. Oil and gas, naval contracts, lots of industry."

"Industry." Callie said the word once again. "He wasn't lying about that."

"He's not lying about anything," Brenna replied. "He's a businessman. I don't think he's out to do us harm."

"We'll have to wait and see," Callie finally said. "It's a done deal. The council approved it even if it was just symbolic. This is more of a state thing—approval, permits, logistics. But they seemed to think eventually this will be a good thing."

Brenna glanced behind them. "Yes, but barely. I thought Mrs. Laborde was going to keel over."

"She's a widow who lives on her husband's pension, and that's very little as it is." Alma crossed her arms and stared at the now-empty council chairs. "I don't know. A lot of new jobs will bring a lot of new people to town. The Fleur Café will be busy. We might have to hire more people ourselves."

"That's the right attitude," Brenna replied. "Think positive."

Callie got up and lifted her shoulder bag onto her arm. "I'm going home."

Her sisters stood, too. "Are you all right?" Alma asked.

"I'm fine. New people will mean new homes, and they'll need someone to help with landscaping and plants and trees and bushes and, you know, I'm an industry. I mean, I run an industry myself. Small scale but…"

"You are a smart businesswoman," Brenna said, latching on to the few good notes in the symphony of fear moving through the room. "This will work out fine. Nick wouldn't work for a man who intended to shut this town down."

Callie walked with her sisters to the door. Outside, the night was sweet with the scent of honeysuckle and jasmine. The wind played against the old oaks while all sorts of scenarios played out inside her head.

She headed to her battered red pickup truck and stood, digging her keys out of her purse. She wanted to get home and into her pajamas and into her bed. She needed to think, to pray. To sleep.

"Callie?"

She closed her eyes and stilled.

Tomas.

"Yes?" She didn't dare turn around.

But she didn't have to. He was there beside her, urging her around. "You left without saying good-night."

"Good night." She couldn't look at him.

Tomas leaned down so she was forced to face him. "You're not too happy about this, are you?"

Finally, she glanced up and into his unreadable eyes. "No. You're shutting down the shipyard with a vague promise of opening it back up. We've heard that kind of vague promise before. It never is good. We need a solid assurance. We need jobs."

He leaned a hand against her car, trapping her too close. "I have my reasons."

"And those reasons are?"

"It's time for a change. I think I can make that change."

"It's you taking over and telling us that we no longer matter," she blurted. "You gave a good spiel and you made a lot of promises, but—"

"I'm not taking over anyone. I don't want to own this town. I don't need this town."

But something in the way he said that made Callie lift her head to stare at him. "Then what do you want? What do you need?"

He stood staring down at her, the moonlight reflecting in his velvet dark eyes, the gray night washing over his intense scowl. His hard, harsh expression softened in the moonlight. "Callie…"

"I have to go," she said. "I work for a living. I have to get up early."

She struggled with her keys.

He grasped her hand, took the keys from her and opened the truck door. Not used to him being so kind, she moved around him and slid into the seat, but he held the door open and leaned in. "I'll see you tomorrow. We'll talk then."

"You don't owe me any explanations, Tomas. You told me this was about industry. And it is. There's good and bad in your announcement. Change is hard on a place that's used to tradition, but we do need some sort of change. So I'm asking you to make it a good one. Don't disregard the people of Fleur. We depend on each other around here, help each other, pray for each other. It's hard on us when an outsider comes in and takes over, even if it is a write-off investment."

"It's progress, Callie. It's business. And that means there are winners and losers."

She took a deep breath and cranked the car. "Well, sometimes progress comes at a high price. And no one wins."

He stood inside the truck door. "Don't leave yet."

She tugged on the door handle. "I have to go."

He finally lifted his hand off the door. "Good night."

Then he stepped back.

Callie didn't dare look at him as she cranked the old truck and backed out of the parking space, but when she was a safe distance away, she glanced in the rearview mirror and saw him standing there staring after her.

This time, he hadn't walked away.

* * *

The sun peeked over the morning horizon in pastels of shy pink and timid yellow. Callie and her crew arrived at Fleur House just as the shimmering rays filled the tall pines and ancient cypress trees along the bayou, casting out a path of light that seemed to absorb the stone-encased walls of the looming house and give them new life.

But she had to wonder if this house would ever feel alive. She didn't think the lone man inhabiting it really knew about real life. But she'd decided not to dwell on Tomas Delacorte and his mysterious ways today.

Pulling her cranky old truck up underneath a just-green tallow tree, Callie got out and waited for the work van full of a half-dozen workers she'd hired to help her oversee this project.

"Gather around," she called, smiling at Pretty Mollie and several younger teens from the church youth group. "Okay, we've talked about your pay and how many hours I'll need y'all. Weekends and after school, of course. This is our first Saturday together, so I wanted to remind everyone of how this works. We'll be here most of the day. My sister Alma will send out lunch so you won't starve. But please remember to behave and work hard. The faster we get this done, the sooner you can go on home and get on with your Saturday-night plans."

"You got any plans, Miss Callie?" one of the teens asked, grinning, his brown eyes twinkling.

Callie had known the kid since his birth, so she was used to his good-natured teasing. "No, David Lee, I don't. Other than finding a quiet spot and reading a good book."

"That sounds boring," blonde-haired, blue-eyed Hannah said, one painted fingernail clawing at her spiral curls.

"You should try it sometime," David Lee retorted. "Reading makes people smart. Oh, I mean some people."

Hannah stuck out her tongue at him. "Then obviously you don't read much yourself."

Everyone laughed at that, except David Lee, of course.

Ah, young love. Callie remembered that. She and Dewayne had sparred and flirted in just such ways when they'd been in high school. And they'd married right after high school and moved into the tiny little house where Callie still lived not far from her papa's house. Life had been good for a few years, but…life had a way of changing pretty fast.

"Let's get to work," she said, turning to open the tailgate of the truck so she could hand out shovels, picks and rakes. "I have a grid that we need to follow. "David Lee, why don't you and the other boys start unloading these plants." She pointed to a spot she'd already tilled and fertilized. "Set them right there and I'll show you the grid once we get our tools in place."

David Lee and the boys started doing as she'd asked while Callie and the girls gathered the tools. "We have a water jug," Callie called out. "And drinking cups. Put your trash in the bag I brought, okay?"

The teens all mumbled and went about their various duties, and soon Callie was knee-deep in mud and manure and magnolia bushes. She tried not to look toward the house, toward that big window where Tomas usually stood. She hadn't seen him since the meeting Wednesday night, but she knew he was somewhere in that big house, making plans for his future empire.

Hannah shoveled soil and shifted on her old tennis shoes. "I've heard a lot about Mr. Delacorte."

"Me, too," one of the other girls said. "My daddy says he's gonna fire everybody down at the shipyard." She stared up at the imposing mansion. "I guess he's filthy rich if he lives here. Daddy says Fleur will never be the same since he moved in."

Callie had thought the very same thing, but she refused to engage in idle gossip. "Girls, we're here to plant not to stir up."

"Is that a joke, Miss Callie?" Hannah asked, a smug look on her face.

"No, it is not," Callie retorted. "Let's talk about something else besides the man who's paying us to do this."

"My daddy said you'd take up for him," the other girl replied. "Since he's paying you so much money and all."

Callie stopped shoveling and stared over at the sassy teen. "Your daddy needs to keep quiet since he has no idea what I'm being paid. I have to work for a living, and Mr. Delacorte needed a gardener."

"Well, your sister works for him, too," the girl said, anger coloring her words. "And she's engaged to that other man, Nick. So my daddy might just be right about you defending him. It's like your whole family is depending on him or something."

"Enough."

They all turned toward the masculine voice that echoed out over the trees and water.

Tomas was standing about ten feet away.

And he was not smiling.

Chapter Six

Both girls lowered their heads and went back to digging dirt, but Callie dropped her shovel and walked toward Tomas. She didn't need him running interference or scaring away her workers, even if they had been talking about him.

"They're just confused," she said. "Don't be angry at them."

Tomas walked right past her to the girls. "Excuse me. Could I have a word with both of you?"

Hannah and the other girl looked horrified. They both blushed a bright crimson. Hannah glanced from Callie back to Tomas. "I guess so."

"Good," Tomas said. Then he lifted his hand and motioned for the other youths. "I'd like to say something to all of you."

Mollie eyed Callie but walked over to stand with the rest of the group.

Tomas's expression looked calculated and full of

disdain. Callie let out a breath and wondered if he was about to fire her entire team.

He gave the girls a long stare then sighed. "I know you've heard some things that are confusing, and I really don't care what you say about me." Then he pointed to Callie. "But you will not accuse or disrespect Mrs. Moreau, understand?"

They all nodded, too in awe to smart off at him.

Callie had to admit, he cut a domineering figure, all tall and arrogant and self-assured. Even in jeans and a crisp button-down shirt, he looked from the manor born.

Tomas asked each of them their names. Then he repeated them back, one by one. "Hannah, Mollie— oh, you're Pierre's Pretty Mollie, right? And let's see—Dana, Monica, Rachel and Jill."

He glanced over to where the boys stood staring in a different kind of awe. "I'll get to you all later."

Tomas gave his full attention to the girls now. He asked them about their families, learned where their fathers worked and discovered that some of them had lost their fathers through death or divorce. He talked about their mothers and their brothers and sisters. He explained how the shipyard had gone down in years past but he planned to bring in a new team to update things and hopefully get it back on track. He assured them that even if their fathers got laid off, they could possibly be called back when work picked up in the next few months.

At first, Callie thought it was an act to put the

girls in their place, but the more Tomas reassured the girls that he wasn't some evil overlord, the more Callie believed him. She watched as the girls seemed to sigh en masse. Then they started smiling, and finally, they started giggling and talking to Tomas as if he were an old friend.

David Lee glared at Tomas, but once he got the boys involved in talk about LSU Tigers football and whether or not the New Orleans Saints would ever play in another Superbowl, things turned all cheery in that corner, too. Several of these boys played high school football. He said he'd make sure to catch some of their games next fall.

So he planned to be around for a while.

Then he summed things up. "When Mrs. Moreau has the gardens and grounds exactly as she wants them, I intend to hold a picnic. And you're all invited. Everyone is invited."

The teens mumbled and chatted about that while Callie stood there shocked. He had repeatedly told Brenna he didn't want to hold a town-wide picnic. What had changed? Probably nothing. Probably this was just a publicity stunt to hold doubters at bay while he worked on shutting down the only major industry in town.

Tomas finished up and then stood back. "So... no more talk about Mrs. Moreau and her family, all right? Anything that happens here is my decision, and you're welcome to contact me if you have more questions. Mrs. Moreau is doing what she was hired to do. She is not involved in my affairs, other than what you see right here." He glanced over at Callie, his eyes holding hers. "And while I admire the way she stood up for me, I don't expect her to fight my battles."

So…he'd come out here to make a point with her, she decided. Tomas Delacorte didn't want others speaking for him. Or about him. She could certainly understand that feeling. But it was kind of him to rush to her defense like a knight shielding his queen. Kind and highly romantic.

Only, she'd decided they had to steer clear of that type of thing. Hadn't she?

After the kids drifted back to their various assignments, she took off her gardening gloves and walked over to Tomas. "So you fight your own battles, right?"

He didn't look at her. "I have, yes, for a very long time now."

She saw the resigned expression shuttering his eyes and felt that strange tugging inside her heart again. "I'm sorry you had to hear that," she said, hoping to draw him out. "But you handled the situation, so I guess that's that."

"That," he said, turning as if to leave, "is just the beginning."

"Did you lie to my youth group?"

"No. But…things will get worse before they get better."

"Because that's what you do—take bad situations and make them worse before they get better, no matter the challenge or the cost?"

His eyes caught hers and Callie saw a barrage of emotions passing through him like a blast of smoke on the horizon. "That's what I do, yes." He stepped closer, his dark hair shimmering as it ruffled his neck. "But…I want you to please trust me, Callie. No matter what, can you do that?"

She wanted to laugh at that suggestion. She didn't trust easily, not since her husband had left her in the middle of a health crisis. Not since she'd decided to live her life free and clear and without any regrets. She trusted in the Lord. That was her kind of trust.

"Sorry, I'm not so good at trusting these days."

This time, she was the one to walk away.

Tomas sat in his office that night, remembering Callie's parting words to him earlier that day. His mother's Bible lay on the corner of the desk. She'd given it to Tomas when she'd gone back into the hospital. She'd died three days later.

"Take this, please," she'd begged. "I know you don't believe, but you'll need God by your side when I'm gone."

His mother, Rebecca, always the faith-filled hopeful. But she'd died a long, horrible death when he had just become a teenager. She'd died without ever telling him who his real father was. But he'd found out on his own and he'd vowed to let that man know that if he'd been there, they might have been able to save her. Without money or insurance, Tomas had felt helpless. So he'd worked hard to never feel that way again.

He was in control now because he had all the power now.

"I know now, Mama," Tomas whispered into the night. "I know and that's why I came back."

He picked up the worn Bible. He'd read many of the passages there, passages his mother had under-lined, her notes written in the margins. Tonight, he turned the page at random and settled on Matthew, Chapter Sixteen, Verse 26: *For what profit is it to a man if he gains the whole world, and loses his own soul? Or what will a man give in exchange for his soul?*

Tomas stared down at the words, a soft electric heat moving through his system. He'd had a grand plan when he'd decided to buy Fleur House, when he'd decided to take over the shipyard. He had in-tended to close the yard down and he'd intended to sell this house to the highest bidder. But…he'd never expected anything or anyone to get in his way, to mess with his head, the way Callie Moreau seemed to be doing.

The minute he'd seen her there in his garden, dancing in the rain, he'd felt a gentle tugging in his heart, a foreign tingling that both amazed and scared him. And changed him.

But he couldn't allow Callie or anyone else to see that change. He should have told those gossiping teens to get out of his yard, but the look on Callie's face had stopped him.

"What profit?" he asked himself now.

He thought he'd give just about anything to watch her laughing and dancing. Here in his home. In his garden. In his life. He didn't understand this pull toward a woman he barely knew, but the feeling was there in his gut much like the feelings he always got when he was closing in on a deal.

"She's not a business transaction," he reminded himself.

This…this was something more, something strong and real and…unsettling.

But was he willing to give up everything he'd fought so hard to accomplish? Everything that had brought him back to the one place on earth he'd hated?

What profit? he wondered.

To win a woman like Callie?

Or to destroy those who'd destroyed him?

Tomas stared at the Bible then got up and pushed it away.

The next Monday, Callie was back in the garden at Fleur House, alone and content. Well, Elvis was with her. After she'd had Elvis awhile, she'd started taking the big dog with her to work sites since some of the yards she worked in were out from town and in remote spots. Elvis could at least alert her if anyone showed up unannounced. Of course, he alerted by making friends with strangers. But it was a form of interference that worked for both of them.

Now, she'd definitely brought him back to Fleur House and hoped he'd make some noise if the French doors leading out to the big terrace opened and Himself showed up to mess in her head and her garden.

His garden, she reminded herself.

But Tomas had pretty much given her permission to do what she wanted with it. He had excellent taste and offered good suggestions or commands, such as his one command regarding the roses, but for the most part, he left her to it.

And Callie so loved being left to her own devices.

Freedom had become precious to her after Dewayne had walked out of her life. Yes, she got lonely, but there was something to be said about being your own boss, making decisions without having someone to question them or scorn them. After she'd survived breast cancer and a lumpectomy, chemo and losing her hair and being sick to her stomach, after she'd survived watching her marriage end, Callie now savored the freedom of each and every day. And the beauty.

So she went on with her day with joy and gleefully dug up the rich dark dirt along a path down toward the bayou and began to plant crisp, fresh gardenia bushes. These would start blooming later in the season, and if Callie had her way, they'd keep blooming for most of the spring and summer.

"There is nothing like the sweet smell of gardenias," she told Elvis.

The big dog lay in a lazy curl near where she'd dropped a burlap sack full of cedar chips. But he acknowledged her obsession with a sleepy grunt.

Callie had just leaned over to sniff the sweet floral scent of a white baby bud when she heard the door squeak open. She looked up and around and watched as Elvis came to life and, in a blur of black-and-white fur, took off to meet the man who owned this particular soil.

She shifted her big floppy red hat and adjusted her attitude. She would be professional and quiet. She would. Really.

"Hello," he called, waving to her.

Callie stood to stare at him. He was wearing jeans again. And a dark T-shirt that seemed to merge with his dark hair.

"Hi." She smiled and called Elvis back.

But Elvis waited for Tomas and then trotted along with his new friend as Tomas moved down the rounded brick steps and strolled toward her.

"Margie and Eunice have made lunch."

"Okay." Callie wondered what that had to do with her. "Then go eat."

"For both of us."

Surprised, she glanced toward the house. "I…I hadn't planned on eating lunch here."

"They went to a lot of trouble."

"That was thoughtful."

"They seem to like you, a lot."

"They go to my church now. Did you bring them from…wherever you came?"

He frowned around the whole yard. "You say that as if I came from another planet."

"Did you?"

His lips twitched. "You have a very dry wit. Are you coming to lunch or not?"

Callie told herself to politely decline, but the words came out, "I could eat, yes."

"Okay then. Shall we?"

"We shall." She hooked her arm in his, amused by his always-formal manners and his carefully cultivated speech. "Elvis will try to eat off the table. Just warning you."

"I have food for Elvis. He'll be fine."

"You think of everything, don't you?"

"I try."

Margie and Eunice must have been watching. The doors immediately opened again and out came the two gray-haired women, carrying trays. They placed the food on the colorful mosaic-tile tabletop and waved to Callie.

"Hello," she said. "It was good to see y'all in church yesterday. Hope you'll come back."

"We loved it," Margie said. "My husband, Bob, has already signed up for the next workday."

"That's good," Callie replied, grinning. "I'm usually in charge, so you might want to warn him that we work long and hard to keep the church grounds pretty." She took off her hat and ran her hand through her hair.

Tomas watched her, his eyes hooded and lazy, as still and observant as a lion.

Callie went on in spite of feeling like a mouse. "We grow a community garden, and we're always needing help with that. I've got to get on that project soon, too."

"He mentioned he'd heard about that," Margie said, her brown curls lifting in the breeze. "He used to grow his own produce, but he's retired now so I'm sure he'll be glad to help."

Callie took note of that. "If he ever wants to work part-time, I'm always needing help at the nursery. I can't pay much, but I do pay."

Margie beamed. "I'll let him know. He likes to piddle, and he helps out around here, too, of course."

Eunice poured iced tea and added fresh mint. "I hope you plant us an herb garden. We like to cook with fresh herbs."

"I did plan to add one." Callie glanced at Tomas. He sat quietly listening to the feminine banter, a smile frozen on his tanned face. "Would you like that?"

His eyes held hers. "I'll like anything that will make life easier for these two."

Well, that was mighty kind of him. And yet another layer exposed. He did have a heart.

She glanced up at Eunice. "Do y'all travel as a pair?"

The two women giggled. "We're sisters," Eunice

replied. "After my Ed died, Margie and Bob asked me to move in with them." Then she looked over at Tomas. "And...since they've been with Tomas for a long time, when it came time to come here, they insisted I tag along."

Margie giggled, but her eyes turned misty. "Tomas insisted, too."

"Like Ruth and Naomi," Callie replied, touched. She watched Tomas's expression soften and her heart seemed to turn to quicksand. "So you brought them all here."

"I was outnumbered," he said, but she could see the pride in his eyes. "Margie and Eunice were friends with my mother."

"We practically raised him after—" Eunice stopped, a hand to her mouth. "Listen to us going on and on. Y'all need to eat your chicken salad casserole before it gets cold. We have fresh strawberries and cream for dessert."

The two women bustled back inside without another word.

But Callie couldn't let it go. "After what?" she asked, hoping to understand what made him tick. "What was Eunice talking about?"

Tomas glanced out into the yard and then lifted his chin toward Callie, his eyes a shielded blue. He didn't speak for a moment or two, his expression taut and tight-muscled. "After my mother died," he said. "Pass the bread, please."

Chapter Seven

Callie passed the bread and watched him butter it, his movements calm and carefully calculated. This man seemed to analyze his conversations and his every move. Had he been raised to be gentlemanly or had he trained himself?

"Tomas?" She waited for him to look at her. When he finally did, she dropped her fork and gave him a direct stare. "I'm so sorry. When did she die?"

He placed the freshly baked bread back on his plate and positioned the butter knife back on the butter tray. "When I was a teenager," he replied. "Heart disease. She needed a transplant but she was way down the list. We didn't have insurance and we didn't have transportation to any state or charity hospitals. Friends tried to help, but...she'd waited too late. She was too sick. After she died, our house was repossessed and I was left with a lot of medical bills. We lost our home."

The summary seemed well rehearsed and blunt,

as if he'd had to tell it so many times he'd memorized the method. And he'd learned not to show any emotion in telling it.

But Callie had to know. "And your dad? Is he still alive?"

He stared down at his uneaten food. "Yes, but I don't acknowledge my dad. Never did. Never will."

In spite of her keen curiosity, Callie tried to hold back on the subject of his father. But she wanted to know how he'd gone from a motherless teen to a successful tycoon.

"So what did you do…after your mother passed away?"

He shoved a spoonful of the tasty chicken-and-rice casserole into his mouth and chewed. Swallowing, he said, "At first, I moved in with my mother's brother and his family in Texas but…we didn't get along. I came back to Louisiana and asked Bob for a job. He and Margie never had any children of their own, so they were willing to give me room and board and some cash as long as I finished school and helped Bob with his construction business. When I turned eighteen I struck out on my own."

Well, that was an understatement. Callie's heart burst with the hurt of knowing that this confident, secure, successful man had once been a hurt young boy without a home, without a family. What could she say to comfort him, to understand him?

"I'm so sorry, but you obviously overcame any adversity you suffered."

He looked into her eyes then, his expression guarded and dark. "Did I?"

Maybe not. "You're self-sufficient now. You can take care of yourself and a whole lot of other people."

Or could he?

"I'm secure," he replied. "I like security. I like being in charge and in control."

Because his life had once been out of control? Callie could certainly identify with that notion.

She ventured into deeper waters. "You said you grew up near here. Where is that, exactly?"

He lifted his fork. "Eat your casserole before it gets cold."

Callie couldn't hide her shock, but she lifted the creamy concoction to her mouth and tried to swallow it. "You don't like talking about yourself, do you?"

"No."

They both ate their food for a moment or two, then he said, "Tell me about your mother."

Should she? Or should she clam up like he had? No, Callie wasn't the tight-lipped kind. "She was wonderful. Always had a kind word for anyone. She was a true Christian. She didn't judge, didn't condemn. She just loved with all her heart."

"You must be a lot like her."

Callie didn't know what to say to that. "I try, but no one can ever be exactly like Lola Blanchard. She was one of a kind." She touched her napkin to her mouth. "People told us after she'd died that God needed her in heaven." She shook her head. "I kind of got tired of hearing that."

His blue eyes flared like firelight at that comment. "Did you blame God for her death?"

"No. I blame cancer for her death. God didn't take her. He healed her, in the only way He could. I've accepted that, but I still miss her. And…I don't need platitudes to comfort me. Sometimes, I just need someone to listen."

He looked over at her, his eyes full of understanding. "I'm a pretty good listener."

Embarrassed, she shook her head again. "I'm not asking you to do that, but I appreciate the offer."

He sipped his iced tea then lifted his gaze to Callie again. "You…had cancer."

Okay, this man was forever shocking her. "Yes, I did. But I survived. Coming up on my five-year checkup soon."

He ran a finger down the condensation on his crystal drinking glass. "And you're healthy, taking care of yourself?"

"I think so. I mean, I try to take care of myself. We eat a lot around here, but we also have a lot of fresh food. Healthy food. If you don't count bread pudding, of course."

He attempted a smile at that, his gaze sweeping over her face. "Alma's bread pudding is hard to resist."

"Yes, it is."

He took another bite of his food. "I suppose you've heard I was married once."

And yet another shocking confession. "Yes, just like me. How 'bout that?"

He sat back and stared across the table at her. "She died."

Callie went for honesty. "I'd heard that, too."

But she wanted to ask him how his wife had died and if that was why he seemed so shut off and cautious. Or if there was something else about his childhood that had shaped him, too.

"We didn't have a good marriage."

Another revelation. "I'm sorry for that, too, then."

"I couldn't help her."

Callie was beginning to wonder if this was a confession or a warning. "You've had some tough times."

"Yes, I have. But so have you."

"We can compare notes."

"No comparing. My wife had issues and they finally caught up with her." He looked away again, out toward the flowing water of the little bayou. "It's hard to help someone when they don't want to be helped."

Callie threw down her white linen napkin and gave up on eating. "Okay, Tomas, I have to ask this because I'm the curious type. What exactly happened with your wife?"

"An overdose," he said, his tone flatlined. "She

was addicted to prescription pain medicine. I tried everything—rehab, clinics, therapy."

So that explained why he'd taken her away. And probably explained why he didn't like roses. Didn't people always send roses, no matter the sickness?

"Oh, my. Oh, how horrible." Callie wished she hadn't pushed him, but at least now she knew the truth. "That's just—"

"Tragic," he said, his face a blank. "What about your ex-husband?"

"What about him?" She sat back up, moved her fork over her food. "He couldn't handle me being so sick. He couldn't handle a lot of things about me."

Tomas lifted his eyes to meet hers. "I can't imagine that."

"Are you being sarcastic?"

"No, I'm being serious. You seem like a dependable, hardworking, loving, lovely woman. What's not to handle?"

A confused heat rushed across her skin. "Well, when you put it that way…"

He leaned forward. "Callie—"

But the door opened and out came Eunice with their dessert. Just like that, the tension left Tomas's face and whatever he was about to say remained unsaid.

"All fresh and chilled," Eunice said with pride as she placed the pretty china dessert plates and two cups of steaming coffee in front of them. "Did you enjoy your lunch?"

"We did," Tomas said, his gaze hitting on Callie with a touch of regret. "As always, the food was great."

Callie thanked Eunice and tasted the strawberries. "This is wonderful."

Eunice gathered their entrée dishes and smiled, a twinkle in her eyes. "Take your time with dessert and coffee. It's a nice day."

After Eunice went back inside, Callie put down her fork. "I should get back to work."

"Finish your dessert first," Tomas said. But the command was gentle. "Don't let me scare you, Callie."

"I'm not scared," she said. "I've always been nosy and curious, so thank you for being honest with me."

He stared at his plate, his own strawberries and cream barely touched. "I want…"

He didn't finish.

Callie watched his face for signs of anger or confusion, trying to understand what he really wanted. "You don't have to explain anything to me, Tomas. I'm a big girl. You and I have been through similar circumstances. We've both been married and we've both lost a lot. That makes us doubtful and cautious." She stood, her need to flee the scene overcoming her need to understand him. "I don't even know what I'm trying to say. I don't even understand what you're trying to tell me." She turned to leave. "Thank you for lunch."

But his hand on her arm stopped her. "Callie, wait."

"What is it?" she asked, her heart bumping a heavy thud, her brain trying to connect the dots. "What do you want to say to me that you're afraid to say? That you can't do this again? That I'm just here as one of your hired people and you don't want anything else from me? I get that. I'm okay with that. I had a bad experience with my husband and… as selfish as this sounds…I'm not looking for anything else. I'm not looking for *anyone* else. So relax. We'll get through this." She looked down at his hand holding her there. "We both know we don't want to go through anything heavy again, right?"

He tugged her an inch closer, his eyes turning a dark blue. "I wanted to tell you… What I wanted to say to you is…your husband left. I stayed, Callie. I stayed. I stayed with my wife until the very end. So I'm not like him." He let go of her arm then. "You need to think about that."

Shocked, Callie could only nod. "All right, I think that's admirable and I'll remember that, but you don't owe me any explanations, Tomas. Now I have to get back to work."

"I'm coming with you," he said.

"What?"

"I want to help you, with the garden."

Callie wasn't so sure about that. She needed some

alone time to digest his doublespeak. "But you don't need to—"

"My estate, my choice," he replied. "C'mon. We're burning daylight." Then he whistled to Elvis and started off down the steps.

Three hours later Callie stood back to admire their handiwork. After she'd called a few of her hired workers to give her an excuse not to be alone with Tomas, they'd planted more lilies, several azaleas, some cast-iron plants and lots of lush ferns and hostas. Callie wanted the long, wide garden paths to be covered with a mixture of different plantings, so she'd spent the afternoon absorbed in that task, rather than thinking about the man who'd insisted on helping her.

"It looks great."

She ventured a glance at Tomas now, remembering their intimate conversation at lunch. He looked adorable with dirt all over his shirt and hands. A fine sheen of perspiration colored his tanned face. He'd worked beside her and the others without complaint and with very little conversation. But just having him near had added a whole new dynamic to the workday.

"Thanks," she said, wondering how she'd been able to concentrate with him hanging around all afternoon. But she had to admit it had been nice having some adult help. He'd been polite to the team, but not overbearing or bossy. "And thanks for helping. You don't have to do that, you know."

"I wanted to help."

The sound of the teens loading up their tools echoed through the late-afternoon wind.

"They sure are ready to get going." He took a quick glance at the finished garden. "Why do you come alone sometimes? I told you to hire as many people as you need."

Did he think she was taking advantage of him? Or maybe not taking what he offered had insulted him?

"I like being alone out here," she admitted. "It's quiet and peaceful and…it gives me time to reflect and talk to God."

He smiled at that. "You talk to God?"

"All the time," she replied. "Don't you?"

"Rarely." He shook his head. "But I'm beginning to get reacquainted with Him since I've been here."

"That's good," she said. "I like that."

Tomas moved closer to her. Out over the water, the sun was beginning to set. Callie watched the shimmering rays piercing through the cypress trees, their heat changing from bright yellow to muted gold. At this very minute, with Tomas standing so near, with her plants and flowers freshly embedded in the ground, she realized two things.

She'd made a mark on Fleur House, left it better than she'd found it, created beautiful colors to surround it and complement it.

She'd also been marked by this place and its new owner. Marked in a permanent way that would bring her right back to this spot and this sunset over and over. This was the kind of memory a person saved tucked away, the kind a person only brought out at special times.

"What a sweet sunset," she said, her heart content and full of an overwhelming thankfulness, even while her knees knocked with awareness. This man made her jittery, but she liked being near him all the same. "I love the sunset over the bayou."

"You didn't want to be alone with me, did you?"

Shocked, she shook her head. "What?"

"You called in reinforcements."

Was she that obvious? "I needed their help."

"We could have done this without them."

"Maybe, but you are paying them to work."

He gave her one of those scowl smiles. "Okay, we'll go with that then."

She dusted her hands against her jeans. "Let's go get washed up."

When Tomas reached out his hand to her, Callie took it and felt the grit of dirt and mud pressed there between them, branding them and changing them.

"You're still scared of me."

"I'm still trying to figure you out."

"Good luck with that."

"I'll get there eventually," she replied with a wink.

He glanced over at her, his expression as golden

and bright at that setting sun. "But time for you to rest now, okay?"

"I will rest. I'll have a good rest tonight. It's nice to be able to sleep after a good day's work."

He nodded at that. "Maybe I'll sleep better tonight, too."

Callie walked with him back toward the big garage where she kept her larger tools. "I hope so. You shouldn't work too hard, either."

"Maybe I should try dancing in the rain," he replied.

"Could do you some good, unless you melt when you get wet."

He smiled over at her. "I think some of the good people of Fleur would enjoy watching that happen."

She stopped a few feet away from her truck. "I know business is about business and we're not supposed to take it personally, but…I wish there was a way to compromise, to save the shipyard. Not just parts of it, but all of it. Everyone here needs a job."

He stared off into the sunset then cut his gaze back to her. "I'm trying, Callie. I mean that."

Callie wanted to believe him.

"That's all I can hope for," she replied. After he helped her close up the toolshed and they'd both washed the grime away, she turned to face him again. "Guess I'll get going."

"See you soon," he said.

Callie called to Elvis and loaded him into the truck. When she backed out and turned onto the long driveway, he was still standing there watching, his silhouette surrounded by the last of the sun's rays. And she remembered his words to her at lunch.

"He stayed," she said to Elvis. "He stayed and watched us home."

Chapter Eight

"Don't cry. If you both start crying then I'll cry and we'll all ruin our makeup."

Callie looked over at her baby sister. Brenna was wearing their mother's wedding gown, but she'd altered it a bit and added some new lace across the bodice. The lace covered Brenna with a demure tease of material that moved down the delicate cap sleeves and came together with one pearl button at the back of her neck.

"I can cry since I'm the oldest," Callie said through a sniff.

Alma nodded then wiped at her eyes. "And I can cry because I'm still a newlywed myself."

Brenna blinked back her tears. "And I can cry because I'm marrying the most wonderful man on earth and I'm afraid I'll do something to let him down, to let both of you down. And Papa—"

"Enough with the letting down," Alma admonished, her hand slapping gently at Brenna. "You are going to have a long, happy life with Nick. And we are going to be two of the greatest aunts ever to your children."

Brenna bobbed her head. "I expect to be an aunt one day, too. Alma, you hear me?"

Alma grinned. "I hear you."

Callie and Brenna both caught on to that grin.

"What?" Brenna asked while her sisters continued to fuss over her dress. "Out with it, Alma."

Alma's eyes grew misty again. "Oh, all right. I didn't want to steal your thunder but…"

Callie clutched Alma's hand. "Are you pregnant?"

Alma couldn't speak. She nodded, swallowed, smiled, cried.

"Oh, oh," Brenna grabbed Alma and pulled her close. Callie put her arms around Alma, touching on the lace of Brenna's dress.

"A baby," she said, the thought of it crushing her with a sweet intensity. "We're going to have a baby."

Brenna stood back to stare at Alma. "Does Julien know?"

"Yes," Alma replied, still blubbering. "We found out last week. I'm six weeks along, and I wasn't going to say anything until after the wedding but…I wanted y'all to know."

"I'm glad you told us," Brenna said, giggling through her tears. "So glad. What a nice wedding surprise."

Callie hugged Alma again. "The best. I'm so happy for you."

Alma found the tissue box and passed it around. "Let's keep it among family for now. I can't believe it. We've only been married six months."

"That's kind of how things work," Callie pointed out. "For some people."

Brenna gave her a sharp look. "You can still have a family one day. Tomas—"

"Is not available," Callie said. "I told y'all about the odd conversation I had with him last week." Well, she hadn't told them everything. For some reason, Callie was very protective of her time with Tomas. She thought about telling her sisters that he'd grown up nearby, but for some silly reason she held even that little snippet of information to herself. "He went through a lot with his wife. I think he still has cold feet in the love department. And to be honest, so do I. Tomas and I are just friends. Very tentative friends."

"But he held your hand. You told us," Alma said while she followed Brenna around, making sure her hair was perfectly styled in an upswept do.

"He did hold my hand and we had a nice lunch and he helped me plant part of the garden and… But that does not make us an item. I'm working for him. Nothing more."

"Tomas is supposed to be here tonight," Brenna reminded her for the tenth time. "And I was supposed to be 'just working' with Nick. Now I'm wearing a wedding gown and he's waiting for me at the front of the church."

"I'm well aware of that," Callie retorted. "And I'll smile and be nice to Tomas, but I won't pin my hopes on him. That's just not fair to him or me." She shrugged, causing her chiffon brides-maid dress to shimmy. "Besides, I like being single. I like being able to do my own thing. Since Dewayne left, I don't get teased or fussed at for going to church, for believing in God, for eating pie, for buying shoes. I don't have to answer to any man, ever again."

Her sisters didn't look convinced.

"It's not about answering to a man," Brenna, newly minted in the wisdom department, replied with a knowing look. "It's about *the man* and fig-uring out the answers together. You know—the one man meant for you. The one God has chosen for you."

"So Dewayne wasn't my chosen one?"

Brenna thought on that. "Dewayne was stupid, plain and simple. But God gave you the strength to see that and now you are free. Free to find *the man*."

Alma shot Callie a quirky glance. "Our little girl has grown up."

"I've fallen in love," Brenna corrected. "And if we don't get out into the narthex, I'm going to miss my own wedding."

"I think Nick will come looking for you if you don't show up," Callie said, deliberately pushing away Brenna's telling comments. "Let's take one last look in the mirror and then…it's showtime."

The three sisters turned toward the wide, full-length mirror in the bride's room just off the main hallway.

"We sure clean up nice," Alma said, smiling over at Brenna. "You look beautiful."

Brenna regarded herself in the mirror. "So do both of you. I can't believe I'm getting married!"

She shot Callie a hopeful look.

Callie looked through the mirror at her sisters. "He said he might start attending church. Tomas, I mean."

"Well, that's a start," Brenna said, smiling back at her with joyous eyes. "And tonight counts toward that, technically."

"It does, yes," Alma agreed. "If he's here, that's a brownie point in the right direction."

Callie prayed Tomas would gain that brownie point. "His wife was addicted to prescription drugs. I think it was an overdose. I think that's why he took her away and...she never came back."

"He told you that?" Brenna asked.

"Yes. He told me the part about the prescription drugs. He also told me that he'd stayed. He'd stayed with her. He said I need to remember that."

"He's in love with you," Brenna said on a sigh.

Callie ignored the lifting of her heart. "And why would you think that?"

Brenna turned to look at her sister without the benefit of the mirror. "He's telling you he'd never leave you the way Dewayne did. He's telling you that he cares, Callie."

Callie pulled away and started gathering their lilies-and-baby's-breath bouquets. "Or he could be telling me he's afraid to care."

Alma fluffed skirts and tidied curls. "I'm thinking he'll dance with you tonight."

"Of course he will," Brenna said, grinning. "He'll dance with you and you'll feel it. You'll see it in his eyes."

They heard a soft knock, then a booming voice. "Is dis wedding gonna start sometime today?"

"Papa," Brenna said, her expression near panic. "How do I look?"

Callie smiled at her sister. "Like a beautiful, happy bride."

"I am that," Brenna replied. Then she kissed Callie and turned to kiss Alma. "I love you both so much."

"We love you, too, sweetheart," Callie said. "Ready?"

Brenna nodded, her eyes misty. "I wish—"

"Mama is right here," Callie finished for her sister. "Right here with us."

"Always," Alma added. She shot a look at Callie, understanding in her eyes.

Because she'd gone with Callie to the doctor two days ago and they were waiting to hear the report on Callie's latest checkup and mammogram.

* * *

Tomas found a seat near Nick's family. He'd rather sit in the back of the church, but Nick had asked him to join the large entourage of Santiagos who'd made the trip from San Antonio to attend the wedding, including Nick's aunt Serena. She'd helped decorate Fleur House, so it would have been an insult to say no.

After shaking hands and waving to Nick's aunts, uncles and cousins, Tomas adjusted his tie and settled back to look at the aged church. The altar was covered in a burst of flowers in shades of pale, creamy whites and yellows mixed in with rich, lush pinks, purples and blues. He smelled the scent of lilies and thought of Callie.

She always smelled like fresh flowers.

He should have stayed away, but he wanted to see Callie in that blue dress he'd heard so much about. Even if he'd tried to scare her way, even if he'd tried to tell her the brutal truth, he knew that sooner or later, he wanted her with him. But he had to keep that revelation to himself because he had to measure it and accept what that might mean in his life. Callie might not want the same thing. She might reject him.

So he waited, his heart trembling as memories of his own ill-fated wedding burst forth with the same intensity as the flowers on the altar. He watched, nervous and on edge, when Nick and his best man and two other groomsmen got into place at the altar. Nick spotted Tomas and gave him a big, happy smile.

Tomas smiled back. And then he turned as a cute little girl and boy came up the aisle, the girl tossing flowers while the boy looked uncomfortable and rebellious as he carried the rings on a satin pillow.

Tomas laughed along with everyone else and then went still.

He smelled her perfume but he didn't dare turn until she walked right by him.

Callie, her hair caught against the nape of her neck in some kind of twist that was covered in the tiniest of white flower blossoms, her dress such a light, sweet blue, it looked like a distant sky.

She walked with a straight-backed regal step, the dress wrapped around her shoulders in soft pleats that seemed to open and flow like cascading water in a sash down her back. Tomas inhaled, his breath stolen, his mind swirling through that mist of sweet, flowery perfume.

He forgot to notice Alma or even the bride. He only had eyes for Callie. He didn't understand how one woman could make him feel so young and vulnerable and filled with anticipation, could make him so scared. He didn't understand why watching Brenna and Nick say their vows could make him hurt and hope at the same time.

But he sat still and watched and listened and he heard the gentle echo of God's voice covering this beautiful, old building in a soft, strong promise. "I am here. I am here."

I am here, Tomas.

Had he only imagined that? Or had the music sounded like a voice? He couldn't be sure. But he felt a sense of peace, all the same. In spite of his doubts regarding his newfound feelings for Callie, Nick had to wonder if it wasn't time for him to come home to his faith.

And when it was over and the bride and groom had pledged their love and promised to honor God in all things, he couldn't understand the tears that seemed to mist in his eyes as Callie walked by.

But he did understand the tearstained brightness that shone right back at him from her sky-blue eyes.

Callie was scared, too.

"He's coming toward us."

Alma's elbow poke caused Callie to jump and gasp. "Well, don't act like we know that."

"I was warning you," Alma replied. "Smile. Act as if you're having a ball."

"I am having a ball," Callie retorted. "The flowers held up, the food is wonderful and our sister is smiling. All in all, a very good day."

"We did it," Alma said, grinning. "And I didn't throw up, not once."

Callie forgot all about Tomas and her sharp-edged need to avoid him. "I'm so excited. I can't wait.

We'll put together a nursery. But which room? The cottage is tiny."

"We'll be okay," Alma said, looking past Callie. "And we'll discuss this later. You've got a bigger fish to fry right now."

"Don't…leave me."

But Alma was already heading in the other direction. Which left Callie standing there like an awkward schoolgirl.

She smelled his expensive aftershave before she knew Tomas was there beside her. Turning, she managed a smile. But the sight of him in a lightweight wool suit and intriguing striped tie held that smile too tightly.

"Hello," he said, his eyes doing a dance over her face. "You look beautiful."

"I bet you say that to all the bridesmaids."

"No, only you. I've been waiting to speak to you all night."

"Oh, something wrong with my work so far?"

"You're off work tonight, but everything is good there." He took her by the elbow. "I think you promised me a dance."

"I don't recall—"

"Or maybe your sisters promised me you'd dance with me."

"My sisters are always messing where they shouldn't."

"Forget that," he said, tugging her along. "Callie, may I have this dance?"

Callie knew she should say no, knew she should run in the other direction. This nice, polite Tomas with a smile was even more disconcerting than brooding, distant Tomas with a frown. But the music was inviting and his smile was enticing, so she couldn't refuse.

Just for tonight, she told herself. *Just for this one lovely, happy night, I can pretend that I'm okay. That I'm happy and healthy and...in love.*

"Yes," she replied. "I'd...like that."

Tomas took her in his arms and held her in such a gentle, respectful way, she felt delicate and precious and secure.

They danced a slow and easy waltz, his hand on her back, his gaze on her. The way he looked at her, his eyes searching and secretive, caused the wall she'd tried so hard to build up between them to crumble like dry clay. Callie didn't want this dance to end.

She didn't understand why this particular man—a man who was brooding and difficult and way too much of a challenge—made her feel so many things in so many ways. She didn't understand why Tomas made her want things she'd decided not to want, ever again. She couldn't reason why she just knew that somehow, someway, they'd wind up together.

Don't make predictions that won't come true, she reminded herself.

But when she looked up and into his eyes and saw that same hope reflected there, she had to wonder if Tomas wanted the same. But maybe he wasn't brooding and surly because he was miserable. Maybe he was afraid, just like her.

Chapter Nine

Callie stood back to admire her handiwork.

"I think we're just about done."

Pretty Mollie grinned from ear to ear and glanced up at Pierre. "We have a lot of talent, maybe even two green thumbs. Hey, Callie, we should plant an even bigger community garden on that vacant lot behind the church."

Callie tugged at her ponytail. "Now that's an idea. Better than that small plot we've been using at the back of the nursery lot, but having it there by the church would show it off more and encourage people to help. The youth group could help maintain it through the summer, and you two could be in charge of that, maybe."

Pierre groaned. "More work out in the heat?"

Mollie gave him a playful shove. "You're not even in the youth group anymore, but you love being out in the heat. You'd get to be the boss—a supervisor of sorts. And Callie did pay us for helping her this week, so we could return the favor."

"I do like getting paid and I don't mind the heat," Pierre, all dark, curly hair and big brown eyes, admitted. "I'd be willing to help in my spare time—with no pay."

"I'd have to rely on volunteers if it's a bigger garden," Callie replied. "But I think we'd get a lot of takers." She remembered Margie's husband, Bob, offering to help.

"I wonder who owns that lot," Mollie said as they began to pick up their tools.

"Not sure, but I can find out," Callie replied. "The church has to mow it and keep it clean, just to keep the varmints away." She took one last long look around, wondering if Tomas would approve. He'd sure kept to himself since the wedding last weekend. Had he decided he didn't want to dance with her ever again? "Let's load up," she called, ready to get home and take a long shower.

Pierre motioned for the half-dozen teenagers who'd been helping and then corralled them toward the nursery van. Callie watched, smiling. Julien's rebellious little brother really had changed over the past few months. She figured Mollie had a lot to do with that. The young man was obviously in love. They planned to get married in a couple of years, after they'd saved up some money and Mollie was finished with her nursing studies at the community college a few miles north.

"Maybe they'd donate the land," Pierre said on a parting note.

"Papa might know the owner, or maybe Reverend Guidry. We try to keep it mowed and clean, since the owner doesn't seem to care all that much about it." After telling Mollie to make sure they'd loaded all their tools and buckets, she smiled over at the girl. "Great idea to expand the garden. And it should be fun to get everyone involved. Alma loves cooking with fresh vegetables, so I'm sure she'll approve."

"And maybe buy some for the café," Mollie replied. "She used a lot of our vegetables last year."

A noise inside the house caught Callie's attention. She wiped at her brow and glanced around. She knew he was up there, probably watching her. That didn't bother her as much as it should have because Callie knew Tomas wasn't a sinister sort of man. He'd taken over the shipyard, true. But he had yet to make a move toward laying anyone off. The whole town was still buzzing about which way the hammer would fall, however. And that worried her.

So far, so good. Or as her mama used to say, "No news is good news."

But for the past few days, Tomas had been avoiding her. They'd danced and laughed and talked at the wedding, but maybe that had been his way of being polite. Maybe he wanted to put on a good front for Nick and Brenna. After all, the man had given them a trip to Paris for their honeymoon.

Was he sincere or did he just like to throw his money around? Had he been nice to her for Brenna's sake? The dance might have been obligatory instead of a mutual thing.

She liked dancing with Tomas, though. And she was pretty sure he didn't mind dancing with her. But that one dance had brought them into a deeper intimacy and had made Callie acutely aware of her growing feelings for him.

That might have scared him away.

Not her puzzle to solve. In spite of the way he'd held her and looked at her while they danced, she had other things to keep her mind occupied and off of Tomas Delacorte and his tragic eyes. She had a business to run and she had a follow-up appointment with her doctor tomorrow morning. She'd been a little tired and cranky lately, but she attributed that to dealing with such a hard-to-read client and dreading her doctor's appointment. Praying she'd have a good report, Callie went about her work. But after Pierre had loaded her delivery van—Elvis included since he'd hopped in with the youths—and they'd all waved bye to her, Callie couldn't help but stop and take one final look at the new landscape surrounding Fleur House.

The big backyard was neat and tidy, with stone paths that wound through beds of colorful lilies and variegated azaleas and old now-pruned camellia bushes. Along the way, wild azaleas and crape myrtles, Japanese elms and magnolia trees lifted to the clouds. Benches, some stone and some teakwood or cedar, sat here and there along the paths. Down by the gurgling back bayou, an inviting wooden swing sat underneath a moss-draped live oak. A sturdy new dock out over the water displayed a wooden pier that was surrounded with built-in benches.

As she rounded the house, she surveyed the front lawn. A cedar-and-stone gazebo stood off to the side, in a spot where the water spilled out toward the Big Fleur Bayou and the Gulf.

She'd planted hibiscus and gardenias around the big, round open building to give it some color. This was her favorite spot, since it had built-in stone benches and an arched, beamed ceiling and offered a great view of both the house up on the hill and the cypress trees and water down below.

"My work here is done," she said, turning to her pickup.

Tomas hurried down the front steps.

"Callie?"

She whirled from putting away her supplies. "Yes?"

Did he see fear in her pretty eyes? Or dread, maybe?

"I…uh…I wanted to thank you, for redoing the yard and gardens. You've done some amazing things with this old, overgrown place."

She beamed a smile but looked embarrassed at his praise. "It's not overgrown anymore. And I found some real treasures hiding beneath all the brambles and bushes." She lifted her right hand and pointed toward the side yard. "Those camellias are sturdy. They come from old roots and they've survived everything from drought to storms. I'll make sure they're taken care of."

Tomas saw the pride in her eyes. She truly loved her work.

"So you'll come back now and then, to maintain things." He glanced around, looking for reasons to bring her back. "I might need some houseplants, too. Margie said something about dish gardens and urns." He shrugged, trying to look helpless.

"Of course." She gave him an impish grin. "It'll cost you, though."

"Add it to my bill." Even if it cost him his heart, he decided. But then, he was pretty sure he'd already lost that to her. "We didn't discuss who would do the upkeep. You shouldn't have to mow this big yard all by yourself."

"Oh, I don't do the mowing," she corrected. "I have people who work for me doing that. They need the money."

Tomas didn't miss the touch of censure in her eyes. "I'm trying to hold off on reorganizing the shipyard for now."

She gave him a measuring stare. "Noble of you. I'm glad to hear that."

She might believe him, but did she believe *in* him?

He turned to leave and then whirled around. "I'll double the pay—for your yard workers."

Callie finished straightening her work tools. "Tomas, you don't have to offer more money every time someone comes out here to help you. We're not the kind of people who need to be bought. We only ask for an honest wage for an honest day's work."

He stepped back, the slap of her words stinging him. "I want to pay people for an honest day's work. This isn't about charity, Callie. I truly appreciate everything the people of Fleur have done for me."

"And we appreciate the jobs," she retorted. Slamming the rusty tailgate, she turned and wiped her hands down her jeans and exhaled a tired sigh. "Just keep things on a business kind of level. People want to work, not be handed something out of sympathy. If you want to impress the people of Fleur, come up with a way to keep most of them working at the shipyard."

Not used to her being so snappish, he noticed she looked fatigued. "I'm not doing anything out of sympathy. When I first came here, I had big plans to cut half the workforce at the shipyard. But I didn't."

Shock colored her face. "Well, I'm thankful for that. You did make a promise to those kids the other day, remember?"

He stepped closer. "I *didn't* do it, but I didn't promise a full work crew, either. That's my point. I could have let everyone go, but I didn't. I haven't decided yet."

She tugged at her ponytail then took a long breath. "You wanted to shut the place down, didn't you? What changed your mind?"

Tomas stared down at her, saw the confusion in her eyes, saw the tug-of-war in her heart. He felt both, but he couldn't stop himself. "You, Callie. You changed my mind." He took another step. "You changed me."

"Me?" She backed away. "I haven't done anything."

"You don't have to do anything. You only have to stand there and be yourself. It's enough. It's…hard to understand, hard to explain. And hard to resist."

Putting on a blank face, she softened her expression and her tone. "Well, whatever I did, I'm glad it worked. You can't fire everyone, Tomas. It's not fair."

"No, but…that's life," he replied. He tapped a hand against the truck. "I need to tell you something. If you'll listen."

"I'm listening." But she looked wary.

"I came here with an agenda."

"You think?"

"I'm not proud of it, but I bought the shipyard to…get even with someone."

He had her attention now. Her eyes flared with smoke and fire. "Who could have hurt you so much that you'd come back here to ruin lives?"

Tomas turned away from the scorn and disappointment he saw on her face. Laying his hands over the tailgate of the truck, he stared out across the prim, immaculate yard. "My father," he said.

Callie let out a gasp. "Your father? Does he live here, work at the shipyard? What's going on, Tomas?"

"I didn't want to involve you," he replied. "I won't involve you. But just know that I didn't follow through with my ambitious need to get back at him."

"Does he live in Fleur?" she asked again, her hand near his on the tarnished truck.

Tomas swallowed the last of his resolve. If he couldn't trust this woman, he'd never trust anyone. "No. He used to live here, but…he's in New Orleans now."

"Tomas?" She reached out her hand toward him. "Tomas?"

"I shouldn't have told you that." He turned to go back to the house.

"Tomas, don't walk away from me. I can be a good listener, too."

He pivoted back to stare at her. "I don't want to talk about this. Not yet." He put his hands in his jeans' pockets. "Callie, remember I stayed with my wife when I could have left. And now, because of you, I'm letting go of some of my old grudges. I don't know why I want to impress you so much, but I do. Just remember that."

"Hey, you don't have to impress me," she called after him. "But you do need to be honest with me."

"I'm sorry." He turned and hurried toward the house, toward the refuge that had turned into a prison. Why had he bought this big old house anyway? To show everyone that he'd gone from being a lonely loser to a successful, wealthy businessman? None of these people even knew who he was or remembered anything about his mother and him, so how could he blame them now?

What did any of that matter if he could never have the things he'd craved all of his life—a home, someone to love, and now, Callie?

What did any of this matter without a woman like her?

Callie toweled her wet hair and tugged her old chenille robe around her shoulders. The shower had soothed her sore muscles, but her nerves were still scattered and on edge.

"His father."

She couldn't get that out of her mind. And she didn't remember any Delacortes living here. Maybe she could do some research and find out the truth. Why the need for revenge? What could a father possibly do to a son to make him feel that way?

Nick had told her Tomas had never known his father. Was that his reason for all of this? To get even with a man who'd abandoned him?

Her cell phone rang and Callie moaned. "No, I just want to eat some soup and go to bed."

But she had to answer. It could be one of her

sisters having a meltdown, or her father needing some company.

Glancing around her plant-filled bedroom, she finally found her phone near her purse on the old oak dresser. She didn't recognize the number. "Hello?"

"I want to take you out to dinner tonight."

Tomas. "Why?" she asked, surprised.

"So we can have some real time together, without teenagers or mud or manure or Elvis. Just us."

The thrill tickling her spine caused her to quip, "I like dogs and teenagers and mud. And I'm used to dealing with…manure."

"I can tell that, but…I want to take you to dinner anyway, to celebrate the garden makeover. You did a great job. Every time I walk through my yard, I'll think of you."

She closed her eyes to that sweet revelation. "I'm not hungry." Her stomach growled in protest.

"Callie, please?"

"Where are we going?"

"Wear something pretty. Your favorite cocktail dress."

"I don't have a lot of cocktail dresses, Tomas."

"It doesn't matter. Just get dressed. I'll come and pick you up."

"Do you know where I live?"

"Yes. You live between your father's house and the nursery, not far from where Alma lives but on the way out of town, right?"

"About two blocks from Alma, yes. The white—"

"The white house with the big front porch that has two ferns by the front door. And an old oak in the front yard."

"That's the house, yes."

"I'll be there in thirty minutes."

Callie hung up, still stunned at how the man had managed to get her to agree to dinner before she'd even said yes.

But…if he was willing to open up to her, to talk to her, maybe, just maybe, she should go to dinner with Tomas.

"God, I know I'm supposed to be Your earthen vessel. I understand I'm supposed to be an example to others who are suffering or in need. But am I the right one for this particular man? Can I really help Tomas Delacorte?"

As she hurried to find a decent dress, Callie stopped and listened to the silence between her heartbeats. And she remembered Tomas's words to her earlier. He'd changed his plans for the shipyard.

"Because of you, Callie."

She prayed that maybe he'd also have a change inside his heart, where he hurt. Could she help Tomas with that?

"Because of You, Lord, I've seen grace and peace. Please let me help Tomas find both."

But she had to wonder, what if it was too late to turn his heart around?

Chapter Ten

Callie immediately called Alma. "He wants to take me on a date. He told me to wear a cocktail dress. I don't do cocktail."

Alma did a little "hmm." "Wear a church dress. You have some really pretty ones from Easters past."

Callie tugged at her wet hair. "They're old. I feel so dowdy and washed-out."

"You are not dowdy, and you surely are not washed-out," her sister retorted. "Wear something floral. You look good in flowers."

"Okay." She hurried to the old armoire in the corner. "How about that one with the boatneck—you know, the sleeveless one with blue-and-green flowers and the full skirt? I have a wrap that matches it."

"Perfect. More lemonade than cocktail, but then you are a lemonade kind of woman."

"Yes. Yes, I am. And if he doesn't like it, well—"

"He'll like it." Alma chuckled. Then she started singing. "Callie's got a date."

"Don't," Callie replied. "And don't call Brenna. She's on her honeymoon. She'd feel inclined to call me and give me specific instructions and that would just make me even more nervous."

"You're no fun," Alma replied. "Call me later. I want details."

Callie hung up and rushed around to dry her hair and slap on some makeup and scented lotion. Then she tugged on the dress and her mother's pearls, grabbed her white kitten-heeled sandals and a shawl and took a deep breath.

Staring at herself in the standing oval mirror, she did a low groan. "Not very chic, but doable."

Elvis sauntered into her bedroom and barked his approval.

She wished she'd had time to put her hair up, but it would just have to twist and curl around her shoulders.

Five minutes later, she heard a knock at the door. Elvis headed that way, his bark low.

Rushing then slowing herself down, Callie took another breath and willed her heart to stop that bashing against her ribs thing. But when she opened the door and saw him standing there in a dark sports coat over a crisp white shirt and with no tie, she had to swallow and talk to her heart again.

The man did dress to impress.

"Hello," he said, his gaze roving over her with what looked like appreciation.

"Hi," she replied, shy now. "Come in."

He did and he took his time glancing around her big open living room. "Nice."

"Thanks." She loved her little craftsman cottage with the mismatched furniture and cozy rooms. It had a lot of nooks and crannies where she could set whatnots and knickknacks right along with fresh flowers and houseplants.

He reached down to pet Elvis. "Your home smells as good as you."

She smiled. "Thank you. Would you like to sit? Do you want some iced tea?"

He shook his head. "No. If you're ready, we can go."

"Okay." She went to put on her wrap, but he took it from her and gently placed it over her bare shoulders.

"You look great."

She turned toward him. "I…I'm not a fancy dresser."

"But you sure know how to wear a dress."

She'd take that as a compliment.

After bribing Elvis into his big dog bed with a treat, she waved bye to her woofing dog and headed out the door, her mind reeling between prayers for guidance and imaginative scenarios for a romantic dinner. And because it had been such a long time since she'd actually been on a romantic dinner date, she smiled and decided to go with the flow. She wouldn't worry about work or her health or her follow-up talk with the doctor tomorrow. Just routine, the nurse had told her when she'd called earlier today. Just to be sure, Alma had assured her.

Please let me relax and enjoy myself, she prayed. *Just don't let me be an idiot, Lord.*

Tomas eased the car into First as he maneuvered it back on the highway. "Are you comfortable?"

"Uh, yes." Callie grinned over at him. "Nice ride."

"Thanks. I thought maybe later we could put the top down and take a drive along the waterway."

"That would be nice." She watched the road. "Where are we going?"

He kept his eyes on that road. "It's a surprise."

"Well, you are a man of mystery."

"You think so?"

"Yes." She turned to him, her eyes illuminated by the dashboard panel and moonlight. "Tomas, thank you for telling me about your father. I won't pressure you, but…I told you I'm a good listener. If you ever want to tell me the whole story."

He gave her a quick glance. "I appreciate that, but tonight, let's just forget about all my baggage and focus on having a nice, quiet dinner."

He intended to focus on her. Callie. In his car. At his dinner table. In his life.

"I think I can do that," she replied, laying her head back against the leather seat. "Or…I might fall asleep. I'm really tired today for some reason."

"You work too hard."

"Don't we all?"

He nodded at that. "Yes. I live for my work, but now that I'll be living in Fleur for a while, I think I'll slow down a little."

"Take some time to stop and smell the roses, maybe?" She put a hand to her mouth. "Oh, I forgot. You don't like roses."

"No, I don't—too many bad memories. But thanks to you, I'll have the scents of jasmine and honeysuckle and gardenias all around me. To remind me of you."

She tilted her head. "That was my devious plan."

He had to laugh at her humor. "Not so devious. But very smart. You make me feel good, Callie."

She gave him an impish smile. "Another part of my overall plan. You need to laugh more, you know."

"Well, you do make me laugh."

She grinned then noticed the road signs. "Hey, we're headed away from town."

"Yes."

Leaning in, she stared over at him. "Are you kidnapping me, Mr. Delacorte?"

"Yes. For a few hours at least."

* * *

When he pulled the sleek two-seater up to Fleur House, Callie turned to face him. "Tomas, what's going on?"

He didn't answer at first. Instead, he got out of the car and came around to help her out. "I'm taking you to dinner, as planned."

Callie glanced up at the house. It shimmered with sweet light as the sun faded behind it and the gloaming came through the fresh evening air. "Well, it does look beautiful at night now. It's not dark and dreary anymore. I see a lamp in the window."

He gave her another searching gaze. "Yes, we have lots of lamps, and Margie and Eunice go around and turn them all on. It occurred to me that you've never seen my home at night."

"Uh, no. I haven't." She let him take her arm. "I've always wanted the complete tour, but I was usually too dirty and muddy to ask."

"You clean up nicely, so I think tonight you can see the whole place." His hand on her elbow, he added, "But right now, let's eat. I'm starved."

"Okay. Me, too." Only she was really too nervous to eat.

When he started toward the gazebo instead of the house, she almost protested. Until she saw the colorful Japanese lanterns someone had strung across the rounded structure.

One little gasp on that.

Then she saw the table set in the middle of the

gazebo, complete with a white linen-and-lace table-cloth, candles and real china and silverware.

Another gasp of surprise. "Tomas?"

"I even sprayed for mosquitoes and set out the Tiki lights," he said in response.

She smelled the citronella right along with the nearby gardenias. "You thought of everything, didn't you?"

"With a little help from Margie and Eunice."

She glanced around. "Where are our chaperones, anyway?"

"Book club," he replied. "At Winnie's house."

Callie also smelled a matchmaking conspiracy. "Oh, I see. Funny, I didn't know Winnie had started a book club."

His eyes twinkled. "Yes. Something about revisiting *Wuthering Heights*."

"Uh-huh." Her eyes pricked with tears. She had the best friends in the world, including her new friends Margie and Eunice. But she'd certainly have to fuss at them for this little setup. "What's for dinner?"

He took her by the hand and pulled out a chair. "Your favorites from what I could find out—shrimp creole from Alma's kitchen, a garden salad with freshly made oil and vinegar dressing, crescent rolls and for dessert—"

"Alma's crème brûlée?" she finished, clapping her hands when he replaced the lid.

"I take it that's a good thing," he said, smiling as

he helped her with her chair. "That one was tricky. Alma insisted we needed to wait until the last minute to burn the top."

So her sister had been in on this, too. And Alma had acted so surprised when she'd called for advice.

"She's a stickler for details," Callie said, still amazed that he'd gone to all of this trouble and that everyone had helped him. "I don't know what to say. I would have been happy with a peanut butter and jelly sandwich."

"Exactly," he said as he sat down across from her and poured some sparkling water into crystal goblets. "You deserve more, Callie."

Callie wondered about that. "I don't think so. I'm content with what I have, most days."

He learned forward to take the covers off their plates. "And what about the other days, the days when you feel as if you might come out of your skin?"

Shocked, she tried to laugh. "Oh, so you have those days, too?"

"Pretty much." He drank some water. "Would you like to say grace before we eat?"

Touched, she nodded. "If I can find the words."

But she somehow did find the words. "I thank You, Lord, for this day, for this beautiful sunset, for this food, and mostly, for this man. Guide us, Lord. Show us the way. Nourish our bodies and our souls. Amen."

When she finished, her throat caught with emotion, she lifted her gaze toward Tomas.

"Are you really thankful for me?" he asked, his expression all humility.

"Yes." She was thankful for him. "And I appreciate this more than you will ever know."

"This is my pleasure," he replied. "I wanted to have dinner with you, to get to know you, since the first time I saw you out here in the rain."

Her throat caught again, tightening with emotion. "Really? I thought for sure you disliked me on sight."

He leaned forward. "I thought that, too. But don't you see it? Don't you feel it? You're a beautiful, smart, talented woman."

She lowered her eyes and stared at her plate. "Funny, I haven't felt that way in a long time. I always seem to have dirt underneath my fingernails."

He took one of her hands in his, studied her fingers. "I don't see any dirt. You have graceful hands."

She pulled away and rubbed her hands together. "I have callused hands. I don't have time to pamper myself."

"Then it's high time you did. Did having cancer cause you to become insecure?"

She lifted her head again, reality clouding out any fairy-tale thoughts. "No, but having a husband who couldn't handle me having cancer kind of messed with my head."

"I'm not like him," Tomas replied. "You need to

remember that." Then he took her hand again, gave it a quick peck and let go. "Now eat your dinner and enjoy being pampered. And when we're finished, I'll show you my home."

An hour later, Tomas guided her up the path to the front door. "Did you enjoy dinner?"

"Yes," she said, her long hair flowing around her face and neck like threads of sunshine. "My compliments to the chef."

He laughed at that. Callie had such a wry sense of humor, it was hard not to laugh. He decided he should laugh more often.

"Your sister is talented, but all of the Blanchard women seem to be blessed with talent."

"Thank you," she replied while she waited for him to open the front door. "I can't wait to see what Brenna did with all the art she purchased for you. She talked about it with such glee. We tried to get her to sneak us out here for a peek, but she refused. She's very loyal to Nick and you."

"She's a good employee. I'm glad Nick convinced her to not only marry him, but to work with him, too."

Callie stared up at the mural as they entered the dining room. "She told me about this. They had it restored. Oh, Tomas, it's beautiful."

Tomas gazed at the big long wall where a scene from long ago played out in vivid detail that showcased a steamboat out in the bayou, men in formal dress and women in colorful, crinoline gowns, and the gardens of Fleur House in full bloom. "I had to get used to it, but it fits the mood of this room."

Callie rushed to the wall, her hand touching on the mural. "I can just picture someone from the Dubois family walking in the gardens like this, long ago."

He stood back, a brush of anger rising up in him like a rebellious wave. "So can I."

She must have sensed his distaste. Callie whirled to stare at him. "Do you like the mural?"

"I like the mural," he said, smiling over at her. "And I especially love seeing you standing there by the mural."

She lowered her head, shy again. "I don't know what to say to that."

She had those moments when she went from being an impassioned gardener to a timid woman. But when she combined the two into the gentle soul that she was, she took his breath away. Tonight, in that demure floral, flowing dress with her hair falling around her shoulders, she looked perfect in his eyes.

Without stopping to consider the consequences, he marched toward her, took her into his arms and lowered his head so he could kiss her. When his lips touched on hers, a great whispering sigh of peace seemed to move through his body. He heard and felt that same sigh in the way she responded.

Her lips felt like home.

Chapter Eleven

Callie lifted away to stare at the man who'd just kissed her. She couldn't speak, couldn't think. Tomas had awakened something inside her that she'd tried to hide.

Her heart.

She'd lost her heart to breast cancer and to the agony of going through a divorce. Once the dust had settled, and she'd survived, she'd given herself a solemn, silent vow to never go through that much trauma again. Ever.

And now she feared she'd lose herself all over again. But her heart couldn't take being broken a second time. So she stood back, her mind in turmoil. Had she wanted this to happen? Hadn't she known that going on an actual date with this man might lead to trouble? To this?

She stared at Tomas now, all the warning signs flashing through her mind like a storm alert. But *that* kiss, now that qualified for a sea full of good sailing.

Tomas must have felt some of the same sensations. He looked hopeful then confused. "Callie?"

"I don't know about this," she sputtered. "I mean, I know that you and I…have kind of been dancing around this…for weeks now, but I'm not so sure I'm ready." She stared up at him again, a choked gulp of an inhale rasping in her throat. "I'm not ready, Tomas."

He put his hands in the pockets of his pants and rocked back on his heels. "I didn't think I was ready, either, but…Callie…I'm not going to make demands on you. And I'm not going anywhere."

She put her hands together, shook her head. "But you're you and I'm…just me."

He grabbed her, his hands gentle on her upper arms. "Just you? You are amazing, beautiful. I'm not playing you, Callie. You don't understand what this means to me."

"I think I do," she replied, shaking her head. "But that scares me. I don't want to feel this way, to depend on you. I can't depend on you."

"Because you think I'll hurt you?"

She nodded and tugged herself out of his embrace. "Yes. And because I'll take things to heart and then, bam, you'll be gone again or you'll figure out I'm not worth your time."

"Don't say that," he retorted, the words sharp-edged. "Don't think you've got me all figured out. Do you know what it took for me to invite you here, for me to finally kiss you?"

She looked down then turned back toward the mural. "If you're feeling the way I do right now, it took courage and guts and a leap of faith."

"Yes. Yes." He inhaled a breath, waited. "Callie?"

Callie turned back to face him. "Tomas, I didn't mean to hurt you or reject you. It's me. I'm scared, so scared." She lowered her head, her eyes downcast. "When I got married, I thought it was for keeps. But…my marriage wasn't strong enough to sustain cancer. My husband couldn't love me enough to get past my operation and my chemo and all the things that go with that." She looked up and into Tomas's eyes. "It wasn't enough for him. I wasn't enough."

He came to her then, taking her back into his arms. "Don't be scared. I won't hurt you. I just want to soak you up like that sunshine you love. Just let me try, Callie. You are enough for me. Please?"

Callie could see the sincerity in his eyes. She knew the cost of that kiss. He was a quiet, tormented man but he'd stepped out of that shell tonight. For her? Yes, for her. Should she push him away or should she enjoy their time together, no matter the outcome?

What should I do, Lord?

Her silent prayer whispered against the night.

What should she do?

Did she deserve to be with this man?

"I don't know."

"Neither do I," Tomas admitted. He took her hand. "Let's walk around the house. Just put that kiss out of your mind and I'll give you the nickel tour. Then I'll take you home. You can think about this—about us—and I won't pressure you. I won't."

He didn't sound so sure.

And honestly, if he tried to kiss her again, Callie wasn't so sure she'd be able to stop him. His kiss had been so gentle, so tender, so rich with promise and warmth and peace, that she wanted to feel his lips on hers over and over.

Patience.

She heard the one word and knew she had to be careful here.

"Okay," she finally said. "We'll just see where things go. But no pressure, no promises, no guarantees."

He gave her a steady stare. "I'll take it."

She smiled, willing her heart to slow down. "Now, let's finish this tour before I change my mind and run out the door."

"I kidnapped you, remember. And it's a long walk back to town."

"Oh, right." She smiled at that. "I guess I have to trust that you'll get me home safely."

"I will," he said. "That's one promise I can keep."

Callie took his hand and forced herself to a scattered calm. "Okay. Where is this sunroom Brenna went on and on about?"

Tomas willed his heart to move from a chaotic beating to a slow simmer. He'd always heard of people feeling an electric awareness when they met someone and fell in love. And after that kiss, he'd certainly felt some sort of charge shooting through his veins, giving him a new life.

Was he overreacting? Being silly? Being foolish?

Maybe all of that and more.

He'd told himself to stay away, to let Callie alone. And yet, each time he saw her he somehow managed to be near her. Earlier today after she'd left, something inside him had gone dark. He missed her being in the garden.

He wanted her here with him more and more, even when against his better judgment. He liked the way he felt right now. He liked holding Callie's hand and touching on her calluses. He wanted this to work, somehow.

But could it work? Could he be the man this woman deserved and still hold on to his need to get even?

I'm in trouble, he thought as he guided her through the rambling house. But he laughed and explained things and showed off rare artifacts and antiques and bragged on her sister Brenna's good taste in art. They moved from downstairs to the second floor, so he showed her the many bedrooms and bathrooms and the dainty sunroom that overlooked the back gardens.

When they reached the sunroom, he stopped. "It's not quite finished, but you can have a look if you'd like. The upstairs balcony is just off this room and I have a smaller balcony off my room."

Callie's eyes widened as she whirled around in the oval sunroom. "I've always wanted to stand on that curved balcony and pretend I'm a princess."

He opened the double French doors into the room with a flourish. "Allow me, Princess Callie."

Her giggle reminded him of tiny bells tinkling on the wind.

"What a beautiful room," she said, her voice full of surprise. She glanced around, her back to the many windows now, and took in the muted walls and the chunky art. Then she stared up at the long empty wall opposite the windows. "You need a portrait right there over that rattan sofa. Something to bring the room together."

He had to smile at that. "Brenna told me the same thing. And I do have a portrait in mind, but the owner isn't ready to sell it yet."

"Oh, I see," she said with a grin. "You figure you'll wear somebody down until they name their price?"

"That's the plan," he retorted, thinking of the painting of her that Brenna had shown him. "C'mon. I'll show you the balcony."

He led her to the next set of French doors and opened them wide. The night shone down on them in shades of moonlight and mauve. The crescent moon seemed to hang suspended over the trees, waiting for them to reach out and touch it. The scent of jasmine and wisteria sauntered through the air. The big oaks swayed just enough to show off the veiled Spanish moss. And out beyond the grounds, the bayou gurgled toward the bay in a soft, never-ending rhythm.

He watched as Callie rushed to the stone balustrades and lifted her head to the sky. She breathed deeply and let out a contented sigh. "It's even more beautiful than I imagined."

Tomas was already half in love with her, but now, right now, standing here with her in the moonlight, he knew without a doubt that he wanted to be completely in love with her. And he wanted her to feel the same about him. But would she once she knew the truth?

Unable to move, he leaned back against a wrought-iron table and enjoyed seeing his favorite view through the eyes of his favorite person. He envisioned her standing just like this for at least the next fifty years.

He imagined going to her, giving her a sprig of flowers and a fresh cup of coffee, then turning her in his arms and telling her how much he loved her.

"Why so standoffish? Tomas?"

Tomas blinked and realized she'd turned toward him, her hand out. "Come over here by me."

An invitation? Or just Callie being Callie?

He walked toward her, his hand reaching for hers. Without a word they stood together, shoulder to shoulder, and listened to the night. Bullfrogs croaking, an owl hooting far off in the bayou, night critters playing through the shrubbery, and the wind whispering a sweet melody through the trees. The night world was alive and thriving and for this brief time, so was Tomas.

Callie turned to him, her eyes misty. "Thank you. Thank you for a perfect night."

Tomas pulled her close and touched his hand to her cheek. "Why are you crying?"

"I don't know. It's just...so beautiful."

He had to kiss her again. He had to capture her essence and hold it close to his heart until he could convince her to come here and be his forever. So he leaned down and drew her near and touched his lips to hers, holding back until she met him and kissed him with a sweet acceptance.

He drew back and brushed at her tears. "We'll take it slow."

"Uh-huh." She feathered his jawline with petal-soft kisses. "We'll get to know each other even better."

"Yes. We have all the time in the world."

"You won't hurt me, will you, Tomas?"

"Never. I'd never do anything to hurt you."

"You don't have to promise me anything. Just... show me."

He held her tight to show her this was real.

When she pulled away this time, she had a new confidence. She drew close and turned to stand with her back against his chest, allowing him to tug her close and hold her with his arms around her stomach.

"I'll never forget this night," she said, her whisper full of hope and awe. "All those times I dreamed of walking through Fleur House, but I never imagined someone like you being here with me. That makes it so much more special."

"So you like my house?"

She shifted and turned back toward him. "It's not about the house, Tomas. It's about the home. All those times I thought about living in this house, that was just a fantasy. But having a life, a real life with someone who understands me and gets me, well, that's not a fantasy. That's a dream come true."

Tomas pulled her around and hugged her tight. "I feel the same. I've lived in lots of places, but this feels like home."

Callie laid her head on his shoulder and they stood there for a long time, absorbing the night, adjusting to each other, doing a kind of slow dance to the wind's music.

"I don't want to go," she said, "but I have a busy day tomorrow."

He glanced down at her, already missing her. "Of course. I had a really nice time."

"Me, too." She took his hand as they strolled back toward the open doors. "Tell Margie and Eunice I appreciate them. Better yet, I'll send them some flowers tomorrow, to show them."

"I'll let them know. And I'll have to thank Alma and Winnie and Pretty Mollie."

"Just thank the whole town since it seems they were all in on this."

"Good idea."

He walked with her, turning off lights and holding her hand tight, his thoughts swirling like that gentle wind. He did have a lot to be thankful for. But he also had a lot for which to ask forgiveness.

Maybe it was time he started paying more attention to all the signals God was sending him.

Maybe it was time for him to begin searching for some sort of salvation instead of plotting for revenge and retribution.

Chapter Twelve

"Your smile is dreamy."

Callie looked over at her sister. Alma watched the road, but she was grinning. "That must mean you had a nice time with Tomas," Alma continued.

"I did." Callie went back to watching the countryside fly by. They were on I-10 headed to her doctor's office in New Orleans. "The food was great, of course. We ate in the gazebo. The night was perfect, cool, with a gentle breeze, candles all around. The mosquitoes didn't bother us."

"I ordered them to stay away," Alma replied. "But forget the bugs. Tell me the good stuff."

"I think I'm in trouble," Callie confessed.

Misunderstanding, Alma shook her head. "It's just a yearly follow-up checkup, honey. You're fine. Nothing to worry about. Dr. Griffin always calls you back in for a chat after your regular checkups, just to reassure you."

"I'm not worried about my checkup," Callie replied. "I'm worried about Tomas. He kissed me."

Alma hit a hand to the steering wheel on her little car. "That's what I'm talking about."

"No, that's not what you're talking about. You can't tell anyone. We decided to take things slow. To be sure."

"How sure do you need to be?" Alma asked, her eyes bright with hope. "I mean, you're happy this morning."

"Remember when Julien decided he wanted you back? You took your own sweet time letting him get you."

"Oh, yeah. Right. I guess I can understand your being hesitant after what you went through with Dewayne. But Tomas is a very decisive man. And it sounds as if he's decided on you."

"We have to see if we can make things work." Callie held back from sharing the intimate details of Tomas's life. She wouldn't betray his trust, even with her sisters. "I just want to be careful this time."

"Nothing wrong with taking time to let a relationship grow," Alma said on a grudgingly positive note. "I hope it all works out for you, Callie."

"Thanks." Callie stared out the window, lost in her own thoughts, until Alma pulled the car into the parking lot at the oncology center. She should be nervous about this checkup, but her mind was full to the brim with thinking about Tomas Delacorte. Could it be possible that he was the real deal?

She went in to see her doctor, her hopes high for a new future. A different kind of future.

When they exited the building two hours later, she was still thinking about Tomas Delacorte. Only now, she was thinking that last night would have to hold her steady for a while.

Because it would be her first and last date with Tomas.

Her cancer was back.

Tomas dialed Callie's number again. He'd tried to call her all day but she wasn't answering. So he left another message.

"Uh, it's me again. I really enjoyed last night. Are you avoiding me?"

Had he scared her away?

So much for a romantic attempt to show Callie he cared about her. Maybe she didn't get into fancy meals and candlelight. But they'd had a good time. He'd kissed her good-night and smiled at her when she'd turned at the door to wave to him. They'd talked about plans for the weekend, maybe a nice drive or a movie.

What had happened between then and now?

Maybe nothing. Maybe she'd just had a busy day, the start of a busy week. Maybe she was out on another landscaping job and had left her phone in the truck.

Maybe. Or maybe he'd pushed things too far last night. Maybe now that she'd had time to think, she'd decided they needed to cool things between them. Maybe she wasn't ready, as she'd said last night. Callie loved her independence, loved being her own boss. And he did, too. But they'd connected last night.

Had he read all the signs wrong?

When his cell buzzed, he quickly checked the caller ID.

Nick.

"Hello," Tomas said, trying to sound chipper. "Why are you calling me from your honeymoon?"

Nick laughed. "Just to tell you that my wife is so thankful for you and this generous gift. We're having a blast. I'm not sure I'll be able to get her to come home."

"We can extend your stay."

"No need. We miss everyone too much. Speaking of that, Brenna can't reach Callie or Alma. Have you talked to Callie today?"

Tomas felt the jolt of unease shooting down his spine. "No, but she is finished with her work here. She's probably moving on to the next project." He wasn't going to share the details of last night with Nick. That was between Callie and him.

"Hmm. Alma should at least answer her cell," Nick replied. "I'll try to call Ramon and see what's up. I don't want Brenna to worry too much, but she calls her sisters on a regular basis, no matter what side of the planet she's on. And they always get back to her."

"I understand," Tomas replied, his gut burning. "If I hear anything, I'll let you know."

A deep dread settled over Tomas after he ended the call. He stood in the kitchen and stared out at the beautiful landscaping that had Callie's stamp all over it. The once-dull yard now held splashes of color highlighted by a rich green carpet of fresh sod. Somewhere off in the house, he heard Margie and Eunice laughing and talking. He wished he could be so carefree, but a dark cloud hung over him like the Spanish moss gripping the old oaks.

He put the phone in his pocket, grabbed his keys and headed to his car. He was going into town to find Callie.

Callie sat with Alma in Alma's cottage behind the café.

"What are you going to do?" Alma asked, her hand holding Callie's. "Papa will suspect something if we don't call him. He's left several messages. Brenna and Nick have called." She scrolled through Callie's phone. "And so has Tomas."

Callie let out a long sigh. "I'll go and tell Papa later tonight," she said. "I have to keep it together for his sake."

"That's right," Alma agreed. "Dr. Griffin did say it was a small lump and that we caught it early. He said a lumpectomy could take care of it. It won't be like last time, honey. We can beat this, Callie. We beat it once. We can do it again."

Callie appreciated her sister's optimism, but they both knew that when their mother's breast cancer had come back the second time, Lola hadn't survived. Callie closed her eyes. The doctor was optimistic, but he couldn't predict anything until they did more tests. And possibly more surgery, a possible total mastectomy and reconstruction, more fear and doubt and sickness and…

Dear Lord, what do I do now?

She opened her eyes. "We'll tell Papa tonight. You and Julien can come with me. Then I'll call Brenna, but we can't tell her the truth until she's home. I purposely didn't remind her before the wedding about this checkup, and I won't spoil her honeymoon." She nodded. "I'll wait a while before I talk to my staff. I'd appreciate it if you don't tell anybody, either. I'll talk to Reverend Guidry. He'll pray for me."

"And Tomas?" Alma asked. "What about Tomas, Callie?"

Callie shook her head. "No. He can't know about this. I don't want him to know about this."

"But—"

She took her sister's hand in hers. "Listen, Alma. The man's first wife died. Died. She was a drug addict—prescription drugs. He couldn't save her. I won't have him trying to save me, either."

"But you're not going to die," Alma said, tears misting her eyes. "I won't let you die."

"You can't make that call, honey," Callie replied. "We both know that."

"I won't let it happen," Alma said. "You'll be okay. I know you will."

"Just don't tell Tomas. I mean it," Callie repeated. "I can't take his pity or his anger. Just let me remember last night without all this…ugliness."

Now he knew something was wrong.

He'd called Callie several times and she had yet to answer any of those calls. He'd gone by the nursery, but her staff had told him she was out on business. They didn't know where she was or when she'd be back. He'd tried the café, but Winnie didn't know where Callie was and Alma had taken the day off. What was going on?

A new thought entered his mind. Had something happened to Alma and the baby? Had she lost the baby? Margie had told him the good news just this week.

Her café employees didn't seem to be concerned, so he dropped that line of thought. Alma had to be with Callie, wherever they were.

Had they gone on a road trip? Skipped town like Thelma and Louise? Or was he just being paranoid?

Shock simmered like a slow boil underneath the myriad feelings moving through him. He couldn't focus on work, had even barked at sweet Eunice when she'd offered him a tea cake. Now dusk was settling like webbed lace over the gardens and bayou.

Tomas threw down the file he was trying to read and stomped out of the house and down to the gazebo. He stood just inside the open structure and remembered sitting here with her last night. They'd talked for hours, laughed at each other's lame jokes, told each other intimate, quirky things that really didn't matter. But being here with her had mattered. Being here with the woman he'd spotted dancing in the rain had awakened all the feelings he'd tried to hide. What had he done to her that she'd turn away so quickly?

Okay, so maybe he was a bit awkward and brooding. He'd worked on improving that for most of his life. Maybe he could be cold and cruel at times. But with Callie, he'd let down his guard, stepped out in faith. He'd been so relaxed and comfortable he hadn't even worried about all of his bad attributes.

But she'd vanished. Hiding from him?

His wife had done the same. When she could no longer deal with his moods and his workaholic mindset, she'd turned from him and found solace in self-medicating. Tomas hadn't been able to save her from her pain. Had Callie sensed that in him? His fear, his hesitation? His inability to truly love.

"What should I do, Lord?"

He hadn't even realized he'd said that out loud until he heard the echo whispering back at him. Tomas leaned his head against one of the sturdy columns, memories tearing through him with a knife-edged sweetness. He had not imagined last night.

That had been real. The kiss had been real. Callie had been here with him, in spirit, in the flesh, in her heart. He'd seen it, felt it, memorized every aspect of their time together.

But he wouldn't call her again and he wouldn't try to find her. He wasn't a stalker, after all. He was just a lonely man who'd finally opened up that protective shield he'd managed to create around himself.

The shield was back now. He'd give Callie time to explain why she wasn't responding, but in the meantime life had to go on. A lesson learned, a risk he'd shouldn't have taken and one he'd never take again. He'd stick to business from here on out. The best risk was a calculated one. Who knew that better than Tomas Delacorte?

He told himself all of these things, but he finally took a long breath and calmed down. Callie wouldn't do this to him. She just needed some time. He could give her that time. They'd both agreed to take things slow.

But he'd have to learn patience in the process.

"What do you mean?"

Callie's heart cracked at the sight of her father's eyes watering. "I'm not sure how bad it is yet, Papa. We have to do tests, get another biopsy and then, possibly more surgery."

She looked toward Alma for help.

"We have to be hopeful," Alma said, her left hand gripping Julien's. "We have to believe Callie will be okay. Dr. Griffin thinks with chemo he can hold off on any radical surgery for now. But he wants to start the chemo as soon as possible."

Papa shook his head. "I know all about okay, girl. I want her to be well and free of cancer. We have to hope for dat, right?"

"Right," Julien said, his expression solemn. "Alma and Callie are gonna fight this, Papa. You know how stubborn they can be. And Brenna, too."

Papa's expression puddled into a frown. "Brenna? Has anybody talked to Daughter Number Three?"

"We're waiting," Callie said, clearing her throat so she wouldn't burst into tears. "I won't upset her while she's on her honeymoon."

"But she's gonna keep calling," Papa replied. "What should I tell her?"

"I'll call her first thing tomorrow," Callie said. "I'm just too tired tonight. I'll tell her I had a busy day today, which I did."

"And I took the day off because I had a lot of morning sickness," Alma added. "Which is true." She glanced at Callie.

Callie could vouch for that. They'd both felt sick to their stomachs after hearing the doctor's report this morning.

Their father stared at them with big, solemn, concerned eyes. Then he inclined his head toward the picture of their mother that Brenna had painted years ago. It hung in the place of honor over the fireplace of his bayou home. "We are gonna beat dis.

You have your mama watching over you, *chère.* So we just gotta batten de hatches and get on with getting you fixed up."

He gave her a big, encouraging smile even while the tears streamed down his face.

"Papa…" Callie ran to her daddy's arms, unable to speak.

He held her close, patting her head the way he'd done when she'd skinned her knee long ago. Then he whispered sweet words into her ear. *"Lache pas la patate."*

Don't let go of the potato. Don't give up.

"I won't, I promise," she replied, tears burning at her eyes. "I'll fight, Papa. I will."

Alma and Julien both hugged her close, too. "We're right here with you," Alma said. Julien winked at her then gave her a quick kiss on the cheek.

Callie basked in the love and support of her family. But her heart ached to be in Tomas's arms, to feel his strength and his support. Last night, she'd finally opened her bruised heart. She'd finally given in to the emotions and the tides that kept pulling her toward Tomas. Had she known today would be different? Had she deliberately tested fate last night, in hopes that today would be a sunny, beautiful, normal day?

Yes, oh, yes. She'd taken a chance and she'd lost.

Last night was just a dream…in an ordinary world. Her world had just gone from ordinary to difficult and trying, frightful. And doubtful. She'd seen what this disease could do to two people. Dewayne had caved under the pressure. She wouldn't watch Tomas do the same.

Please let me survive this test, Lord. And please give me the strength to stay away from Tomas Delacorte.

Because he deserved a second chance with someone who could be there with him for the long haul.

Chapter Thirteen

A week had gone by.

Tomas had not heard a word from Callie.

He roamed the big house at night, thinking about her. During the day, he threw himself back into his only salvation—work. He went back to what he was so good at—brooding and buyouts. But he couldn't forget that one night and having Callie in his arms.

He'd given up on calling her. She did not respond to his calls and the only explanation he could pick up by casually asking was that she'd gone to New Orleans for a few days of rest and relaxation. That almost made sense because she'd worked hard on his property for weeks now. She deserved a break.

But why hadn't she mentioned it to him or at least called to let him know?

Had Callie left because of him?

He stayed away from town, determined to go back to his solitude. But unlike before, his solitude was now a torment rather than a comfort. He read books but hardly remembered the words. He listened to music but barely heard the lyrics.

Eunice and Margie shadowed him, worried, concerned, frightened. They'd seen his black moods before. But they had not seen him this dejected and brooding.

Tomas realized just how bad things had gotten when Eunice brought in a lunch tray and left it by the door, rather than bringing it to his desk and staying to chat awhile.

Tomas stared at the soup and sandwich and the glass of iced tea. On a side dish, the ever-present cookie lay warm from the oven. They always remembered his sweet tooth.

He stared at his computer screen then got up, walked past the tray and headed down the hallway to the kitchen. He heard them whispering in hushed tones but kept walking.

They both looked up, shocked and unsure, when he rounded the open arch from the hallway.

"Oh, hello," Margie said, scurrying to look busy. "Did you want more tea, another sandwich?"

"I can get you something else if you'd like," Eunice added.

"No, nothing. I'm…fine." Tomas motioned to the big chunky pine table. "Let's sit."

Both women did as he asked, their expressions filled with concern. Margie brought the plate of fresh-baked cookies with her, a soft smile pasted across her wrinkles. Eunice got the coffee, her brown eyes filled with a hopeful light.

Tomas waited for them to find their chairs then leaned forward, his gaze on the sisters who'd lived next to his mother and him and had taken care of him for so long. Even Margie's husband, stodgy old Bob, had helped him along when he'd been at his worst. At least Bob had the good sense to get out of the house. He'd gone into town to repair a porch for an elderly lady.

"Are you gonna fire us?" Eunice asked, her fingers twisting a frayed dish towel.

"Did we do something you don't like?" Margie asked, her hand on the sturdy table.

Tomas shook his head and pushed a hand over his hair. "I'm not firing anyone. I came in here to apologize to you. I'm sorry I've been so moody lately."

Margie shot Eunice a pointed glance. "I told you he wouldn't fire us."

Eunice shrugged. "We were part of the conspiracy."

"What conspiracy?" Tomas asked. "What are you talking about?"

"We helped set things up for your big date with Callie. We thought—"

"You thought Callie and I would hit it off and that she'd come around more and more?"

"Yes." Margie bobbed her head. "Did we do something wrong?"

"Not you, but me," Tomas replied, glad to have

someone to talk to. "I think I said or did the wrong thing. She's not talking to me now."

"Have you been into town to see her?" Eunice asked.

"I tried to see her after our date. But…she's never around when I happen to go by Callie's Corner."

"She's a busy woman," Eunice said. "But she should come out here to check on the place. She needs to make sure this landscape will hold. You should call her and remind her of that."

"She finished her part," Tomas said. "Maybe when she's finished with a project, she's really finished."

Margie gave him a sympathetic smile. "Callie's not that way, Tomas. She liked you. We all saw that. It must be something else."

"What?" he asked, truly wanting to know. "What else could it be? Do you think she's figured out who I really am?"

"We didn't tell her," Eunice replied, shaking her head. "We haven't mentioned that to anyone. We haven't told anyone that we used to live next to you, either."

Margie broke a cookie in half. "As far as I can tell, no one knows you're related to the Dubois family."

Relief flooded over Tomas. "Let's keep it that way."

Eunice handed him a cookie. "But…maybe if

you did talk to Callie and tell her the truth, maybe she'd understand."

"I can't do that," he replied. "I'm not ready for that."

The sisters fell quiet, their expressions full of both disapproval and understanding. And loyalty.

Tomas stared out at the sloping backyard. The brilliant colors hurt his eyes. He couldn't talk about this anymore. He had to get over Callie. "I'm sorry I took things out on both of you," he said, standing. "I'm going to eat my lunch now." He grabbed an extra cookie just for show.

"He's eating again," Margie said to Eunice. "That's a good sign."

"Silly, he never stopped eating," Eunice retorted. "But he did stop smiling."

"I can hear you," Tomas called with a wave of his hand.

"We know," they said in unison.

That did make him smile. Where would he be without Eunice and Margie and Old Bob? They'd protected him from an early age and he'd never forgotten their kindness. They would remain in his house, under his watch, for as long as they needed.

Determined to get on with his life, Tomas took his tray out onto the terrace. Settling on one of the black wrought-iron chairs, he took a bite of the chicken salad sandwich and tried not to think about days when Callie was out there in her floppy hat, Elvis by her side. This was his garden, after all.

Then he thought up a new tactic. He could always call her and file a complaint. Callie would come running if she thought her work was below par. He hurried through his lunch then headed out into the yard. He had to find something that would bring Callie back out here to check on her work. And once she was here…well then maybe he could talk to her and find out what was really going on.

But an hour later, Tomas was even more frustrated than ever. The place was as perfect and pristine as Callie had left it over two weeks ago. Tomas stood there, his hands on his hips, surveying the immaculate gardens. She'd placed trails everywhere, so anyone who came to Fleur House could stroll among the azaleas, crape myrtles and dogwoods, or smell the lilies and the magnolias. The scent of Confederate jasmine and newly budding gardenias wafted through the air. Wisteria threads bloomed up in some of the old pine trees, their vines clinging tightly. Callie had insisted on leaving a few of the old roots so the wisteria could decorate the backyard.

He watched as a blue heron walked gracefully through the shallows down by the new dock. A fine lady enjoying his garden in her own lazy way. The graceful bird only added to the natural beauty that Callie had nurtured and pruned and weeded and cleared.

She'd also done that to his heart, too.

So why had she suddenly decided to avoid him?

When someone tapped him on the arm, Tomas almost jumped with joy, thinking it might be Callie.

"She's in town, working at the community garden," Margie said, her tone knowing. "I mean, she's watching everyone else work at the community garden. Bob's there and just called me. There's a big lot beside the church that she wants to use to grow vegetables, but the owner's playing hardball about selling it to the church." She leaned in. "Bob says Callie looked tired and frazzled when he saw her there earlier."

"How much?" Tomas asked, hope rising like the tide out in the bay.

Margie named a price.

"Do you know who owns the land?"

"Sure do. We all do. Bob's tried to convince him to let it go at a fair price, but…he wants the money more than he wants to do a good deed, I reckon."

"Do you have a number where I can reach him?"

Margie bobbed her head. "We've all got that man's number. He lives on the edge of town, out toward the shipyards."

Tomas followed Margie into the house and waited while she found the phone number. Pointing to the information, she said, "He's a real estate agent, so his signs are all over the place."

Tomas nodded, thanked Margie then got in his car and headed out to the edge of town.

* * *

Callie stood surveying the beginnings of the meek little garden they always planted behind the church. She was late in getting started this year, but they'd have beans and peas, tomatoes and cucumbers and several other vegetables in a few weeks. She was disappointed that Mr. Tillman refused to part with the half acre of land right next to the church.

But then, she'd been disappointed in a lot of things lately. She had to get this done before she went into New Orleans for her first round of chemo. Her summer would be a rough one, with treatments every two weeks. She'd been through another biopsy, but at least no major surgery for now. She was thankful for that.

So it was either plant in the old, smaller garden or have no vegetables to share for the rest of the summer. Besides, she needed something to do to keep her mind off of cancer and...the man she couldn't forget.

She went over the grid with Bob and the other volunteers. "So, tomatoes, corn, field peas, butter beans, okra, green and red peppers, hot peppers. Did I forget anything?"

Bob pointed to the tender shoots sitting on the bed of the old pick-up. "Potatoes and turnips. And herbs. You know how much Alma uses fresh herbs."

"Yes. Margie and Eunice requested those, too." Callie stopped when they heard a motor rumbling. Tomas. Pulling up to the church office.

What was he doing?

Her heart beating enough to shake her ribs and remind her of the sore spot where her doctor had done the biopsy, she turned and regarded the dirt for all it was worth. Maybe he wouldn't notice her out here.

"Let's get busy then," she said on a shaky voice, her emotions as clotted and dry as this unearthed soil. She started barking orders like there was no tomorrow.

And in her case, that might become the truth.

When she heard the motor revving again a few minutes later, Callie glanced up and watched as Tomas took off in the other direction. He'd never once glanced her way.

What was he up to, anyway?

A few minutes later, Reverend Guidry came out of the office with a big grin on his face. "Y'all won't believe what just happened," he said as he jostled up to the group.

Bob gave Callie a wink. "Tell us, Rev."

The minister rocked back on his heels. "He really didn't want anyone to know, but since y'all just saw him leave…Mr. Delacorte just bought old man Tillman's lot and then donated the whole space to us for our garden."

"He did what?" Callie had to sit back on the tailgate of her truck. "Are you sure?"

Reverend Guidry nodded. "Oh, yeah. Very sure. He paid Mr. Tillman with a check—a mighty big check. They did a gentleman's deal and shook on it, but Tomas said he'd have the lawyers make it all legal. But we can start digging over there. Like right now."

Callie couldn't believe what Tomas had just done. How could she ever thank him? And why had he done it without so much as a word to her?

Because you've hurt him, she told herself. *Because you've shut him off without an explanation. He did it to show you in the only way he knows that he still cares.* And she still cared, too, even if his act of kindness had involved throwing around a lot of money. At least this was for a good cause.

But he hadn't bothered to come and tell her himself.

Of course not. She'd been rude to him without any explanation. But…she couldn't talk to him, couldn't see him now. She'd fall into a heap if he so much as looked at her.

Nice to know he could be so kind, and it was sweet of him to do, but Callie reminded herself that in spite of his good deed, she couldn't have a relationship with Tomas. It wouldn't be fair to him.

She'd rather hurt him now than get closer to him and cause him a horrible kind of grief later, the same grief he must have gone through with his wife. Callie didn't want Tomas to stay out of some sort of misguided obligation.

"Let's refigure this and get busy over there then,"

she said, smiling in spite of the pain arching through her system. "We've got some land to clear."

Reverend Guidry gave her a sympathetic smile. "You need to thank Tomas, Callie." He'd also encouraged her to tell Tomas the truth.

"I will," she promised. "One day very soon."

That day came sooner than she'd imagined.

Tomas Delacorte came to church the next Sunday morning.

She should have known it was him when she heard the whisperings and rustlings that always occurred when someone new walked into the church. But she'd been so involved in reading the bulletin, so involved in trying not to think about Tomas and how much she missed him, that she'd completely missed his entrance.

But when all eyes seemed to move from her to the aisle behind her, Callie turned around to find him heading straight to her pew, *his* eyes clearly centered on her and only her.

Papa, looking worried and pale, gave her a long, hard stare. She knew that look. He was wondering when she planned on telling everyone about her illness. Papa wanted as many prayer warriors on the case as possible.

While Callie only wanted to be done with it.

Alma poked her in the ribs, a hopeful look on her face. "Do you see what I see?"

"Yes," she said on a hiss of a whisper. "What should I do?"

"Pray?"

"Funny. I've done that already. A lot."

"Well, God might have heard you. And maybe He's giving you the answer right now."

"Not the answer I was looking for."

"Hello, Tomas," Alma said, smiling up at the man standing there, waiting for Alma to move over.

"Alma." He looked past her to Callie. "Is this seat taken?"

"No," Alma replied before Callie could find her tongue. "In fact, I'm waiting for Julien. I'll just move down so you can sit here, by Callie."

Callie wanted to throttle her sister, but she was in the Lord's house, after all, so she couldn't commit any acts of violence. Instead, she waited for Tomas to sit down then she looked straight ahead.

"Hello," he said into her ear, facing forward.

"Hi." She looked down at her hands. Her work-worn hands.

"You've been avoiding me."

"Yes. I mean no, not really. I've been busy."

"With your big garden behind the church?"

"Yes, that and well, it's that time of year. A new spring."

"You don't bluff very well, Callie."

She finally looked up and into his eyes. What she saw there tore through her system. He looked frustrated and confused. His eyes were an angry storm.

"No, I'm not good at hiding the truth. And…I was going to call you to thank you for what you did the other day. We've already started on tilling the new acreage. We hope to plant the garden on Good Friday."

"I'd like to help out."

"But…you have work of your own."

"And I'm the boss, so I can take a few hours off here and there."

"That's not necessary."

"I want to help."

"Okay."

The organist started playing a loud rendition of "Love Lifted Me."

Tomas leaned close, his breath tickling at Callie's neck. "We need to talk. Can I take you to lunch after the service?"

Callie didn't know what to say. Should she go to lunch with Tomas and tell him the truth? Or should she tell him she wasn't interested and watch him walk away?

"We'll talk later," she replied, motioning to the choir.

So they sat in silence, Alma and Julien and Papa on the pew with them. Alma kept leaning forward to check on Callie, her expression a mixture of curiosity and concern. Callie tried to focus on the sermon, but Tomas was close, so close. Close enough that she remembered being in his arms, remembered kissing him, remembered how sweet and gentle he'd been as they'd moved through his house, as he'd taken her heart.

Reverend Guidry talked about a perfect heart, a heart for Christ. "This kind of heart forgives our sins," he said, his tone low and dramatic. "But before we can have our own perfect heart, we have to be open to God's love and grace. We should have a gracious heart, a forgiving heart, a heart that understands, a heart that takes a risk for love's sake."

A perfect heart.

A risk for love's sake.

Callie thought about that and wished she did have a perfect heart, but her heart was bruised and battered and scarred and hiding. Yes, she was hiding her heart. She couldn't take that leap of faith, that risk of opening herself up to pain.

Was she trying to protect Tomas? Or herself?

She didn't want her heart to be broken again. She didn't want to watch another man walk out of her life because of her illness. So she prayed that God would give her the strength she needed to get through this next phase of her life. Without Tomas.

I might not survive here on earth, Lord. But I'll fight until the bitter end. Don't take me yet. Just let me live to be around him. Just near him. For a little while. Like now, having him here in church with me, so near.

She inhaled the clean, soapy scent of Tomas

and thanked God for getting him this far into the fold. Before she could get things clear in her whirling mind, the sermon was over and everyone was standing.

Tomas turned to her. "Well?"

She looked around for an excuse. "I… We usually have Sunday lunch with Papa, out at his house." She swallowed, prayed. They'd have to be careful what they talked about. She hadn't told many people about her cancer.

Tomas frowned at her silence. "I really need to talk to you."

Callie decided she had to talk to him, too. "Would you like to join us?"

Surprise sparked through his eyes. "Is that your way of avoiding being alone with me?"

Yes. "No, not at all. I just don't want to disappoint Papa. If you can't come—"

"I'd love to eat Sunday lunch with your family— that is, if you can stand me being there."

"I don't mind," she said, warming to the idea even though her hands were cold with fear. "You did us a big favor and your good deed deserves a good meal, at least."

His eyebrows lifted like the wings of a hawk. "That's mighty gracious of you, but I didn't do it to impress anyone. I did it for you. You don't need to repay me."

Callie didn't know what to say other than a whispered "Thank you." His eyes told her he wanted more than gratitude.

A gracious heart. Yes, she certainly had that. She wanted to take Tomas by the hand and run away. Run as fast as she could to a place that was safe and gracious and comforting and without pain or illness. A place where they could walk through the garden, hand in hand, with no worries.

But instead, she nodded to him. "I can never repay you for what you did, but…I'd like you to come and eat with us."

He followed her out of the pew, seemingly unaware and untouched by the prying eyes all around them. "Will you and I have a chance to talk? Alone?"

She hoped not. "Maybe. We'll have to see."

"Yes. We certainly will."

Tomas felt out of place in this long, mismatched cottage by the water. The house was an interesting maze of add-ons and porches. Rather charming if he weren't so nervous and edgy. This was a family house, full of love and laughter and life.

While his stone mansion up on the hill was a cold, drafty museum of a place—lovely but silent. Unless Callie was there, of course.

"More mashed potatoes?" Mr. Blanchard gave Tomas a pointed look then shoved the bowl toward him. "You don't need any fancy manners here, Tomas. Just need to be hungry."

Tomas slid a sideways glance toward Callie. "The food is wonderful, as usual. You have a lovely home."

Mr. Blanchard grunted a reply. "It suits my needs."

The tension threading through the sparse conversation made Tomas think he probably shouldn't have crashed this meal. Everyone in the room seemed coiled and ready to snap. Mr. Blanchard's expression was etched in sadness. Maybe worry? Julien and Alma, both usually talkative and pleasant, only spoke in muted tones and glanced toward Callie.

Did they resent him being here?

"The roast beef is good," Julien said to no one in particular.

"Alma always cooks a mean pot roast," Callie replied with a forced smile.

Tomas noticed the portrait over the fireplace. "You resemble your mother," he said to Callie. Then because he didn't want to offend Alma, he added, "You all do."

"*Oui,* dey sure got dere *maman's* genes," Mr. Blanchard said on a low chuckle. But his eyes held a hint of grief.

Julien filled in the silence. "And her spirit." He winked at Alma. "Independent thinkers, are these Blanchard girls."

Alma shook her head and looked down at her plate. "We're trouble, that's for sure."

"So I've noticed," Tomas said, giving Callie another glance. "Sweet but stubborn."

Mr. Blanchard let out a hoot of laughter. "Well, you've met all of my daughters so now you know." His smile disappeared while his gaze moved to Callie.

Tomas smiled, glad Callie's father had lost the mantle of sadness. "Yes, I have. Talented bunch."

Callie frowned as she stood. "Okay, time for dessert."

Mr. Blanchard's smile softened. "What did Daughter Number Two bring for us today?"

Alma grinned at her father's question. "Strawberry shortcake—freshly baked sweet yellow cake with strawberries straight out of Tangipahoa Parish. Whipped-cream topping." She followed Callie into the kitchen.

"Wow-wee," Julien said, pumping his fist. "I'm so glad I married the cook."

Alma laughed out loud. "*Oui,* and your stomach is beginning to be glad, too. Which is why this dessert is low-fat."

Both Julien and Mr. Blanchard looked shocked.

"Make mine a double," Julien said in the voice of gloom.

Tomas saw the love shining through in their banter and figured their solemn moments came because they missed Lola, the matriarch of this family. He stole another glance at Callie. She was busy cutting cake and piling on strawberries. She looked natural, standing in the kitchen, still in her Sunday dress but barefoot now, her hair curled in a loose chignon, so prim and proper. Except for the stubborn golden strands that refused to be contained. Those loose tendrils framed her face with a curling, beckoning rebellion.

He still cared about her, still wanted to be with her, but he had to understand why she'd become so distant. Maybe because he'd held her in his arms, felt the current that swirled around them with the strength of a tugging tide. Maybe because she'd turned away and seemed determined to stay away and he needed to understand why.

Callie and Alma whispered in sisterly conspiracy in the kitchen while Julien and Mr. Blanchard plied Tomas with questions about the shipyard and his other properties here.

"Are you buying up dis town?" Mr. Blanchard asked with a glint of dare in his eyes.

"Not all of it," Tomas replied. "Just the parts I want to own."

"Why do you want to own property here?" Julien asked while the women passed out the dessert and poured coffee.

Tomas studied Callie to see her reaction. She gave him a quick glance then sat down beside him. The woman was certainly hard to read.

"It's what I do," he finally explained. "I wound up in Texas and acquired a lot of property near Dallas and then moved on to San Antonio. It kind of became my thing. I made a profit and kept at it. Now I buy companies and turn them around."

"Then sell them again, for a profit?" Julien asked between bites of cake and strawberries.

"Yes. That's the American way."

"Are you going to sell Fleur House?"

Tomas turned at Callie's question.

"That depends," he said, his fork resting on his dessert plate.

"On what?" Alma asked, her tone challenging. She glanced from Tomas to her sister.

Tomas stared over at Callie. "On a lot of things." Then he bit into the rich shortcake and tried to swallow the lump in his throat. "This is good," he managed to croak.

Callie gave him a measuring gaze then dug into her own dessert.

Did she realize everything depended on her?

Thirty minutes later, Tomas stood out in the backyard waiting for Callie. She'd told him after dessert she'd show him the rest of the property. Mr. Blanchard had gone to his bedroom for his Sunday nap and Julien and Alma had gone home so Alma could rest. She was getting tired a lot more these days, they'd explained with smiles. Because of the baby.

A baby. Tomas was happy for Alma and Julien, of course. But he had to wonder if he'd ever find a family of his own. He thought of Callie and pictured her holding a tiny infant.

His heart did a spin of longing.

Callie would make a wonderful mother.

"Hey."

He turned to find her walking toward him, still barefoot, her floral dress whispering around her long legs like wildflowers unfolding in the sun.

"Hello." He waited for her to join him out by the bayou waters where he'd found a black bistro table and two wrought-iron chairs.

"Want to sit?" she asked, her head down.

"Yes. If you want to. Or should I go? I don't want to disturb your father's nap."

"No, stay awhile. Papa's a heavy sleeper."

Tomas waited for her to sit then did the same. "You have a nice family."

She gave him a direct stare, her eyes full of some mysterious something that he couldn't pinpoint. "Yes, I do. We're close." She glanced across the water to the shoreline on the other side. "Tell me about *your* family."

That question threw him off balance. He didn't like to talk about his so-called family. "Not much to tell."

"But you said you grew up near here. You must have moved away when you were young."

"I was thirteen when I went to Texas."

"Just you?"

"My mother had died. Remember, I went to live with my uncle."

"I see."

But he could tell from her questioning eyes she didn't see.

"That didn't work out so well, so I came back and stayed with Margie and Bob for a while. It's a long story and...right now I'd rather talk to you about something else."

She leaned forward, held her hands folded in her lap. "You want to know what happened with us, right?"

"Yes." He watched her, wanted her to explain. "Callie, I didn't mean to scare you. I'm sorry I pushed too hard, too fast. But...don't be afraid of me. I...I enjoyed being with you. I'd like to see you again. Don't avoid me, okay? If you're not ready, if you're not interested, I'll understand. But don't shut me out. I...I value our friendship."

She looked shocked at first, but then her expression changed to somber and quiet. Resolve. He saw a quiet resolve there in her high cheekbones, in her determined eyes. He also noticed a dark fatigue around her eyes. "Callie, what's wrong? What are you not telling me?"

She sat back and took a deep breath. "I value our friendship, too. I'm sorry I pulled away. I just needed to think this through. I don't want to make another mistake."

Relief washed over him. There was still a chance. "I understand. Neither do I."

She lifted her head at that statement. "But...you

loved your wife. You were devoted to her until the end."

He nodded, closed his eyes to the memories. "Yes, I stayed with her until the end. But…I have a confession to make."

"What's that?"

"I didn't love her the way I should have."

Callie opened her hands and held tightly to the arms of her chair. "But…you told me you stayed with her. You tried to help her."

"I did," he said, getting up. "We got married very young and…we loved each other, but things started changing after we'd been together a few years. She couldn't have children and she became bitter and distant." He turned from the water and looked down at Callie. "This was during my start-up years so I worked a lot of long hours. She became more and more depressed and before I knew it, she had become dependent on prescription drugs."

Callie stood and came to his side. "Did you stop loving her after you realized she was addicted?"

He shook his head. "I don't think I ever truly loved her, not in the way I should have. I tolerated her because I was infatuated with her. She was beautiful—dark hair and eyes. But she'd always had this sad, somber disposition. It matched my own. In the end, we became toxic to each other. The love was gone from our marriage long before she died."

Callie put a hand to her mouth. "That's what you tried to tell me over and over. You stayed with a woman you didn't love, out of duty and a sense of obligation?"

He lifted his head and looked into Callie's eyes. "Yes, I did. I owed her that much at least."

"Yes, yes, you did," Callie said. But he saw the shift in her, saw the fear returning to her eyes. "That must have been so hard on both of you."

"The hardest thing I've ever done." He twisted away to focus on the distant shore. "I couldn't abandon her."

The bayou ran a greenish-black, a soft gurgling that took it toward the big bay. A splash down the way and the sound of ducks quacking broke the silence that had fallen between them.

"I don't want to live like that again." He turned to face Callie, but she had sunk back down onto her chair. She looked pale, so pale. "Callie, are you all right?"

"Yes. I'm fine. I…I think I just need to go home and get some rest."

"I'll drive you."

"No, no. I have my car." She got up, held to the table. "You go on, please."

"But—"

Her eyes told him to leave. "Tomas, we're good friends and I appreciate you worrying about me. But…we can't take this any further. I'm not ready to do that. If you need me for anything, for the gardens and the landscaping, just call."

Anger and doubt robbed him of his sense. "And you'll send someone out to fix things?"

Guilt colored her face. "Yes. Or if I'm not busy, I'll be there myself."

"Right. Thanks for lunch." He turned to walk back up toward the house, his heart sputtering and grinding.

Why had he told her the truth? He'd come here to find out what was wrong with her and instead, he'd poured out more of his secrets to her. And by doing so, he'd managed to push her even further away. What would she think if he told her all of his secrets?

They could never be friends. Because he wanted more. And he'd thought by opening up to her he'd be able to help her get past her obvious doubts. But the whole conversation had taken a bad turn. Was she disgusted with him for his inability to be a good husband?

He wanted her to understand that he had fallen for her.

And he knew in his heart that she had feelings for him, too. What he couldn't figure out was why she'd suddenly decided to deny those feelings.

Chapter Fourteen

"He doesn't want to go through that again."

After making that declaration, Callie stared up at Alma. Two days after Tomas had told her his deepest fear, she still couldn't bring herself to tell him the truth.

Alma's sympathetic gaze turned to understanding. "So if you tell him about your cancer now, you think he'll feel obligated, the same way he did with his wife?"

"Yes." Callie shrugged. "Even though all of this is new to us—the feelings we have for each other—we can't take things any further. It would be hard for both of us."

They were at the Fleur Café, waiting to have lunch with Brenna. She and Nick were home from their brief stop in San Antonio to see Nick's parents and now her sisters wanted details from the honeymoon. She'd promised pictures, too.

Callie had to tell Brenna about her diagnosis.

Alma was there for support. "I won't go through that again, either," Callie said now, her voice low. "I still remember Dewayne's eyes when...when he realized my body had changed after surgery. He looked confused and disgusted, but underneath all of that, he was terrified. He gave up. He gave up on me and our marriage. I'm only beginning to know Tomas, and I do have feelings for him, but... it's too early in our relationship to dump all of this on him. If he can be a friend, that's great. Nothing more right now."

Alma tapped her unadorned fingernails on the table. "But you don't know how he'll react, Cal. He might surprise you."

"No, he'll do exactly what he told me he did with his wife. He'll stay. He'll feel obligated to...pretend he cares. I can handle friendship, but not pity or duty. I'll get through this and then we'll see."

The door opened and in breezed Brenna, her hair caught up in an antique clip and her smile beaming. Callie envied the happy glow on her sister's face. *"Bonjour,"* Brenna called, smiling and laughing as she waved to everyone with a just-arrived-from-Paris attitude.

Callie and Alma both hopped up to hug her. "We missed you," Callie said, holding back tears.

"Sure did," Alma added. "You look great. You look—"

"In love," Callie finished, a shard of longing piercing her heart. "Now sit down and tell us everything."

Brenna snuggled into the booth and took a breath. "Well..."

She stopped, her eyes on Callie. "What's wrong?"

Callie gave Alma a pleading glance. "Nothing. Keep talking. Where are the pictures?"

"On my iPad," Brenna said, her chin jutting out. "What's wrong?"

Alma nodded to Callie. "We want to hear about you first."

Brenna sat back, a stubborn glint in her eyes. "What is wrong? Is it Papa? The café? Alma, is the baby okay? Oh, did something happen at the nursery? Wait, it's about Fleur House, right? Was Tomas rude to you?"

Alma glanced at Callie. "The baby is fine. We're all fine."

Callie grabbed her sister's hand. "Tomas was a perfect gentleman, honey. I've finished there and he approved my landscaping."

Brenna's brows lifted. "And?"

"And nothing. It's not about him."

Brenna looked skeptical. "But...you and he... didn't hit it off?"

"We're friends," Callie said, trying to practice the standard line. "Just friends."

Brenna looked disappointed. "Is that all? Is there something else?" She stopped again, a hand going to her mouth. "Your checkup. I told Nick it was almost time for your five-year checkup." She grabbed Callie's hand. "You're okay, right? Callie?"

Callie shook her head, dread bearing down on her like a heavy weight. "No, honey. But I will be. Soon."

Spring moved through Tomas's garden like a floral blanket unfolding over a bed. The vibrant colors and perfumed scents made a dramatic backdrop for the newly renovated mansion.

The big, lonely, newly renovated mansion.

He missed the sound of Elvis barking out by the bayou, missed Callie's laughter floating over the trees. He even missed the rowdy youth group and their ability to tune out the world with earplugs and a little player full of music.

Tomas wished he could drown out the world. Or at least get Callie out of his head. He wanted to call her so he could hear her voice. But he refrained from that. He'd discovered the only way he could see her was at church.

A safe haven.

So he went to church to be near Callie and in the process, he actually began to listen to Reverend Guidry's sermons. He also listened to the chatter of church ladies and learned a lot about this community from asking questions of the old-timers. The initial resentment they'd shown toward him was gradually fading, to be replaced with a grudging respect.

And he was beginning to hold a grudging admiration for this little town.

Which only added to his woes. When he started making the cuts at the shipyard, that attitude could change. But for now, he could hold off on that awhile longer. After talking with some of the employees, he'd been to the shipyard and watched them work, had met with them to come up with solutions. His original plan of taking over and stripping down the once-vital, vibrant industry had now shifted. He'd consider all suggestions, but he still needed to stick to his agenda.

But tonight, he'd forget about work for a while.

Tonight was Wednesday devotional and potluck at the church. Good fellowship and good food, as Reverend Guidry had put it.

"Son, when you got those two things in life, you are indeed a rich man."

Tomas had believed he was already a rich man. But the jolly minister had a point. What good was being wealthy when you didn't have food and fellowship with other human beings?

Or with the woman you wanted to have food and fellowship with? The woman you wanted to spend more time with?

So he turned from the balcony and straightened his casual button-down blue shirt, then headed downstairs. He was going to find the kind of nourishment that seemed to ease the pain of being alone.

Margie and Eunice were waiting at the portico to the garage.

At the sound of Tomas's footsteps, they both turned.

"Hey," he said, determined to keep walking.

"Where you headed?" Eunice asked, grinning.

"Same place as you," Tomas replied.

"We're waiting for Bob to get the car. Want a ride?"

"No. I'm taking my car."

He heard feminine whispering behind him.

They still held out hope that Callie would come around.

He wanted to hold out hope, but he was beginning to think that maybe God had other plans for him. And here he'd thought he planned things for himself all the time.

His plan for tonight consisted of being in the same room with Callie. But when he got to the church, he couldn't find her. Alma walked by, her head down, carrying a platter of fried chicken.

"Hello?" Tomas hurried to help her. "Let me."

"Thanks," Alma replied after he'd taken the serving pan. "This isn't that heavy, but Julien watches me like a hawk." She patted her growing tummy. "I'm a lot stronger than I look."

"I can believe that." He waited, looked around.

"She's not here," Alma replied, her expression sympathetic.

"Oh, okay. Night off?"

"She…uh…had some work to do at home."

Tomas shrugged. "I just wanted to say hello."

"I'll tell her."

He sensed Alma wanted to say more, but she turned and hurried away.

Over the next hour, Tomas ate his food without tasting it and tried to focus on the devotion lesson that centered on Easter. When he bumped into Nick at the dessert table, he glanced around again. "Where's Brenna?"

"With Callie." Nick's expression changed. "I mean, I think she's with Callie."

"What are those two up to?"

"Who knows? You know women. Probably looking at our honeymoon pictures." After a little small talk, Nick hurried away.

Tomas wondered if he had the plague. Seemed the entire Blanchard clan and spouses were steering clear of him.

Was Callie's family avoiding him because she couldn't take things any further with him? Or were they still upset about him taking over the shipyard?

Reverend Guidry came to sit beside Tomas. "All alone tonight?"

"You noticed?" Tomas held up his tea glass. "Just me and the other bachelors." He motioned to the two senior men sitting down the way. They both looked to be in their eighties.

Reverend Guidry laughed. "Give it time, Tomas. You're young and free."

"Free." Tomas glanced over at the preacher. "Free."

"Yep, that's what I said."

"There is something to be said about having your freedom, I guess." He was remembering what Callie had said to him, about being her own boss, about being free and independent and making her own choices.

Was that why she was afraid to take the next step?

He shot up out of his chair so fast, it grated across the floor and scared one of the older gentleman so much he almost dropped his fork. Tomas excused himself from the table.

He was going to Callie's house.

"Here's a warm cloth, Callie."

Callie lifted her head and took the towel Brenna offered her. "Thanks."

"Can you make it back to bed?"

She nodded, too zapped from throwing up to say anything. Chemo was never kind. She'd hoped this time she'd be able to tolerate it more but apparently being older didn't make her any stronger.

Brenna helped her into bed and pulled the chenille spread up over her. They both knew the chills would come now.

"You don't have to stay," Callie said, dragging her hand down the soft blue chenille. "Go home to your new husband."

"I'm staying until Alma gets here," Brenna replied. "Just rest, okay?" She adjusted the covers again. "Do you want some soup?"

"No." Callie closed her eyes and prayed the worst was over. But she knew this would get worse before it got better. She touched a hand to her hair. Not yet. Not yet. She dreaded that the most. Losing your hair so your body could get well didn't seem fair. But cancer was never fair.

She let the fatigue take over her body and tried to drift off to sleep so she wouldn't have to think about things to come.

She thought of Tomas and the moonlight she'd seen in his eyes the night he'd held her. What a sweet memory. A memory she could hold and relive over and over. It held her, soothed her and broke her heart all at the same time.

A cool spring wind pulled through the screen of her open bedroom window. Callie pulled the cover close and enjoyed the fresh air she always craved. A knocking sound jolted her out of her sleep. She jumped, but Brenna was right there. "Probably Alma, though for the life of me I can't believe she'd knock. We never knock."

"True," Callie whispered. They all had an open-door policy.

So who could be knocking at her door at nine o'clock in the evening?

Tomas waited for the door to open, prepared to spill his words before Callie shut him out. But Callie didn't open the door. Instead, Brenna stood there, shock and surprise coloring her face.

"Tomas."

"Hi, Brenna." He searched the room behind her. "Is Callie here?"

Brenna came out on the porch and closed the door. "She's asleep."

"This early?" Tomas could tell Brenna was hiding something. She looked as worried and guilty as a kid who'd gotten into mischief. "Is everything okay?"

"Yes. Fine. She's just tired. Long day at work."

Tomas didn't believe that. Callie had more energy than anyone he knew. "Okay. Well, will you tell her—"

"Bren?"

He heard the weak call through the open window. "Is that—"

"I'm coming," Brenna said. She turned back to Tomas, her hand on the open door. "I have to go. I'll tell Callie you stopped by."

When a crash sounded through the house, Brenna looked panicked. "I have to go, Tomas."

Tomas went from concerned to let-me-in-now mode. He sprinted past Brenna and headed toward the room where he'd heard the sound.

"Callie? It's Tomas. Are you all right?"

No answer.

He hurried down the hallway and pushed at the

partially open door to what he assumed was the master bedroom. "Callie, I'm coming in."

"No!"

He heard the feeble cry but it was too late. He rushed into the room and found her on the floor, a broken glass that must have held water beside her. The rug was wet.

"Callie?" He lifted her up and checked her for cuts or bruises. Shocked at how pale she looked, he turned to Brenna. "We need to call 911. She's not well."

Callie rolled her head back and forth. "I'm all right. Just go, please. Brenna?" She tried to sit but seemed too weak.

Tomas went into action, lifting her into his arms so he could get her back to the bed. "Brenna is right here," he said, trying to comfort her. "You need a doctor."

Callie opened her eyes and searched the room. "Brenna?"

"I'm here, honey."

Tomas saw the tears in Brenna's eyes. "What's wrong with her, Brenna?"

She didn't speak. She kept staring at Callie.

"Brenna?" Anger clouded over his fears.

"I'll tell him," Callie said. "Give us a few minutes."

"Are you sure?" Brenna asked, her husky whisper hard to hear.

Callie nodded. "Go."

Her sister left the room but kept the door open.

Tomas turned back to Callie, touched her damp forehead, saw the gray pallor that colored her usually rosy face. "What's wrong with you?" he asked, even though he'd pretty much figured things out. Even while his brain refused to accept what his eyes could see. "Callie?"

She stared up at him with lackluster eyes. "My cancer is back. I…I didn't want you to know."

Tomas's world tilted. The darkened room seemed to stifle him. He couldn't breathe, couldn't think. But now, now he understood why she'd turned away from him. Now everything made perfect sense. He had to swallow, had to inhale. Touching a hand to her face, he stroked her hot cheek over and over, until he felt her teardrops on his fingers. And then she took his hand, held it tight there against her skin. For a moment, her eyes met his, clear and precise and relieved.

"Callie?"

The moment faded and so did the hope in her eyes.

"Leave," she said, pushing his hand away. "Just go. I don't want you to see me like this."

"Callie?" He swallowed, pulled her up into his arms. "I can't leave. I can't. Let me help you."

"No," she said, rolling herself into a tight little

ball. "No. It's just the chemo. Bad week. I'll be better soon. Go."

He heard Brenna. "Tomas, you need to leave, okay?"

He shook his head, turned back to Callie. "Callie," he whispered. "Callie." He kissed her cheek, tasted the salt of her tears, and after a few silent minutes, got up and left the room, his heart shattering with each step.

Chapter Fifteen

Callie sat at her kitchen table a few days later. It was early morning. She loved watching the sun come up over the bayou. The golden pink rays stretched across the dark water like an arm reaching out to hug someone.

She thought of how Tomas had held her the other night, his fingers stroking her skin. When she'd first woken up the next morning, she'd thought she'd dreamed the whole thing.

But Brenna had reminded her that it had been real.

"He was stunned," Brenna told her the next day. "I don't know how to describe it." She'd taken Callie's hand in hers. "I think the man cares, Callie. A lot. He sat in your living room until well past midnight. After I explained things to him, he sat so silent and still. He looked crushed. He didn't want to leave."

But Alma and Brenna had finally told him to go home.

And he'd told them he'd be back.

But that had been days ago. Had he changed his mind after realizing what was happening? After understanding what had become her reality? She couldn't blame him. She didn't want to put Tomas through this. She wouldn't put him through this.

Callie shifted, sipped the soothing hot cinnamon-and-ginger tea Alma had brought over with some freshly baked blueberry scones. Glancing over the weekly *Fleur News,* she kept the beautiful world just outside her door in her periphery as she read the latest news she'd been missing. At least she was feeling better today. So much better that she intended to go in to work at the nursery for the first time in four days. Now that everyone knew her cancer had returned, she had nothing to hide.

Now that Tomas knew, she had to face him and get on with her life. Without him.

But he was everywhere, including in the weekly newspaper. A long feature article about the Fleur Shipyard caught her attention. Funny, but she'd forgotten that the Dubois family owned the shipyard. Or had, before Tomas had bought them out.

Or forced them out, according to the rumors.

The article went on to say that the last remaining Dubois was in an assisted-living home in New Orleans, but there were relatives scattered here and there all over the country. It appeared that Tomas Delacorte had found most of them and had bought up their shares, one by one.

Callie figured that was the way huge business contracts happened. Tomas must have worked many long hours to find all those people. Which made her believe he really wanted that shipyard. But why? The man was already rich. Maybe he just liked to stay busy and productive. Or maybe he enjoyed shutting things down so he could rebuild them from scratch.

And maybe she needed to stay away from articles about him.

When a truck pulled up to the garden lot across the road, she stood and took notice, hoping to get her mind back on her own business. The entire church had taken up the cause for her community garden, but the volunteers usually didn't show up this early in the day. It was barely past six in the morning.

She didn't recognize the truck, so she watched, curious to see who climbed out of the bright blue vehicle. But when the driver finally stepped down and shut the door, she let out a little gasp of surprise.

Tomas Delacorte. In a dark T-shirt, jeans and heavy work boots. He went to the back of the truck and took out a garden hoe and clippers and some other tools. Had he come to work on her garden?

He glanced over toward her house and Callie ducked back out of the big bay window in her dining room. Taking another sip of tea, she was glad this was a good week. She felt almost human this morning. And she had already decided to venture out after her tea and scones.

She hurried to her bedroom and rushed to get dressed. She wanted to help Tomas with that garden.

Tomas turned away from the little white house down the street. He knew she was in there, resting, maybe watching. Brenna had grudgingly kept him informed.

"She has good days and bad days, Tomas. Just give her some time. One thing I can tell you about Callie. She moves to the beat of a different drummer. When she wants to come back out, she will."

He'd tried to reason with stubborn Brenna. "I can help her. I can sit with her and make sure she gets to her treatments in New Orleans."

Brenna had thanked him and smiled. "I'll keep that in mind." And maybe out of pity for him, she'd added, "In fact, I'll put you on the list for backup on the days we might all be busy."

Tomas felt helpless, shocked, shattered. But he realized the Blanchard sisters were a proud lot and that they'd drop everything to help Callie. They took care of their own. He was an outsider, an interloper, but he wanted to be a part of that tight-knit family. He wanted to help the woman he'd fallen in love with. Whenever he thought of Callie dancing in the rain and then remembered her suffering, he wanted to scream and fight someone. It wasn't fair. It was never fair.

Margie and Eunice had commiserated with him at breakfast on Monday morning. "They announced it in church Sunday and asked for prayers," Margie said. "We plan to do a fund-raiser for her. You know the cost of all of this is ridiculous. She has a little insurance, but…"

Eunice finished up there. "We hear last time her whole family pitched in and helped with the cost. The whole town helped as much as possible. Everyone loves Callie."

Tomas could understand that concept. But he knew better than to offer to cover the cost of her medical bills without waiting to talk to her family about how to make that happen. So he did the next best thing. He intended to cover all the good deeds she did for this community. He intended to pitch in wherever he was needed. Because that's what Callie would do.

And besides, hard work kept his mind off the question that hung like a black cloud over his head.

Would she make it this time?

He understood why she'd shut down her feelings for him. She had a bigger battle to fight now. And while it stung that she didn't think he could handle that battle, he planned to show her that he could take whatever the future had to dish out.

He intended to prove that to Callie, somehow.

Tomas looked at the fresh green shoots sprouting through the earth in straight, symmetric lines and picked a row. Then he started hoeing the weeds and tilling the soil. He wanted to see this garden grow and mature and he wanted Callie to be here when they harvested the first crops.

After a few minutes, two more volunteers showed up. Bob, with Margie and Eunice, came next. Then two more and then another and another. People started showing up, and with a nod and very few words, went to work on what was now being called Callie's Garden.

Tomas finished the row of butter beans and turned to start on the okra when he looked up and saw Callie slowly making her way across the street. She wore her big floppy straw hat and a button-down shirt over khaki pants. Beautiful as always.

Without thinking, he dropped his hoe and headed over to meet her.

"Hello," he said. He took her by the elbow and watched for traffic. Her arm felt fragile and delicate to his touch. Had she lost weight? "How are you?" he asked, praying for good news.

"Not so bad today." She gave him a weak smile. "I'm sorry I scared you the other night. I somehow managed to knock the water glass off the night-stand. Dizziness does that to a person."

"You don't owe me any apologies," Tomas replied, a simmering anger hidden underneath his relief at seeing her.

He wouldn't be selfish by fussing at her because she'd kept this from him. But he could be disappointed.

Callie turned to him when they'd made it across to the garden. "But I do owe you an explanation. Maybe we can sit down and talk later?"

"Of course." He guided her to a bench centered underneath a towering live oak.

"I don't want to sit and watch," she said, tugging away to greet people. "I want to help plant."

"But you're—"

"Not an invalid," she retorted as she pulled heavy work gloves out of her pocket. "I'll let you know if I get tired, I promise."

"Okay." Tomas wasn't sure how to deal with a sick Callie. She'd always been so vibrant and full of gusto. Seeing her this way—pale and gaunt, with dark circles underneath her eyes—made him want to hold her tight and never let her go. But he knew he had to tread lightly here. He didn't want to patronize her. Callie wouldn't like that. And yet, he didn't want her to overexert herself, either.

"Do you need some water?" he asked.

"No." She smiled and waved to several other people. "I need to get down on my knees and play in the dirt."

Tomas smiled at that. "Okay. The cherry tomato

plants need clearing and pruning, according to Bob. The weeds are sprouting all around them."

Callie nodded and made her way toward where they'd planted the tomatoes. "I'll get right on it."

Tomas watched her then glanced around to notice that others were doing the same. No wonder she hadn't wanted anyone to know about her cancer. People treated you differently when you had a deadly disease. He could see that in the way people either avoided looking at her or asked her intimate questions that bordered on being rude. But he left her to her own devices for the rest of the morning. Every now and then he'd stop what he was doing and find her down one of the rows. She'd look up and smile at him, the not-so-fragile patient reassuring the broken grown man.

As long as he had her where he could watch over her, Tomas might just make it through this.

By eleven o'clock, Callie's strength was beginning to wane. She slowly made her way over to the bench and took a seat. The cool morning breeze had turned into a sunny hot wind. She was perspiring and she felt light-headed, but she was also content and thankful.

"Hi."

She turned to find Tomas there with a bottle of water. She took it and drank deeply, enjoying the coolness of the liquid on her throat. "Sit with me," she suggested, moving over.

Tomas sat and drank from his own half-full bottle. "I think we're done for today. The garden looks good."

"You had a lot of helpers," Callie replied. "Thanks for doing this."

"They came to help you, not me."

She wished this confident man could see that he mattered, to her and to this town. "But you took the first step. Or rather, grabbed the first hoe."

He laughed at that. "I haven't worked in a garden in a long, long time."

"Did you have a garden, growing up?"

He looked away, off toward the west. "Yes. Out of necessity. We had to survive somehow."

Callie wanted to ask him about his family, but she didn't voice her questions. She didn't want to mess with the fragile peace that had settled over them. Before she could say more, friends stopped to tell her goodbye. Soon, everyone was gone and she and Tomas sat alone.

"Are you hungry?" he asked, his gaze moving over her face.

"Maybe some soup." She tried to stand.

Tomas was right there, helping her up. "Wanna go to the café?"

She glanced across the street toward the Fleur Café. "Sure. Since Alma and the entire staff have probably been dying to see what we're up to, let's save them some time and energy while they try to figure out if we're an item or not."

He laughed at that and made her heart do a somersault. When this man laughed, it was pure enticement and enjoyment. Callie decided she'd make him laugh as much as possible while he was here today.

"Are we an item?" he asked as they made their way to the café.

She wanted to say yes, but she couldn't let him think they even had a chance together. That would be too cruel for both of them. "People will talk, no matter what. But we know the truth."

They were at the door when he turned and asked, "And what exactly is the truth between us, Callie?"

Callie stared up at him, wishing with all her might that she could let go and tell him her worst fears. But…he knew what she was dealing with and he knew her future was iffy at best.

"I think you know the answer to that," she replied.

Then she was swept up in hugs from everyone in the café.

While Tomas stood there, still and quiet, pondering the brutal unspoken things they had to face.

He asked for a table out on the back porch so they could have more privacy. Now at last, they were alone. Tomas had watched and waited patiently while Callie assured her many friends that she was feeling better.

Now the sun was warm on the deck and the

mocking birds were chirping and fussing in the redbud trees.

Callie looked up at him and smiled. "Sorry about all the attention. Everyone is trying hard to be positive, for my sake. So I have to stop and reassure them."

Tomas wondered at that. "How do you reassure them when you can't be sure?"

She looked puzzled then gave him a direct glance. "Whatever happens, I can reassure them that I'll be okay. No matter what."

She was telling him that she'd be okay if this new round of cancer killed her. He understood that but it didn't mean he had to like it. "But you will fight this, right?"

"Of course. I'm not giving up, but I'm preparing."

"Prepare for the worst, hope for the best."

Her smile seemed so serene. "Prepare for eternal life but work hard in this one. Always."

Tomas leaned back, his fork edging the slice of praline pound cake Alma had brought out for dessert. "Why didn't you tell me right away?"

Callie traced a finger around the rim of her dessert plate. "I think you know the answer to that question, too."

"I want to hear it from you, though."

She shook her head, tossed her ponytail. "This is hard enough, Tomas, without going into details about my feelings for you."

"Then you do have feelings for me?"

She lifted her head, her eyes dark with longing and regret. "Yes, but—"

"But your cancer is back and so that means you've put everything on hold? You've put us on hold?"

"Yes. I need my strength to fight this monster, so don't make me fight you, too."

"I never wanted to fight," he said, leaning close. "I only wanted to be with you."

"Even like this?" she asked. "Have you thought about that? I mean, really thought about it?"

"I've thought of nothing else since the night I kissed you," he said, anger coloring his words. "Were you testing me that night?"

Confusion blushed across her face. "Testing you? For what?"

"If you'd already been to the doctor and if you even suspected what he'd discovered, you could have told me your fears. Why didn't you, Callie?"

The look in her eyes tore at him like rose thorns. "Isn't it obvious? I didn't know for sure that night that my cancer was back, but no matter what, I wanted one night where I could enjoy being with you. If I'd told you my concern then, we wouldn't have…"

"We wouldn't have kissed each other," he finished. "But I would have known. I could have helped you, comforted you."

"You can't fix this, Tomas. No one can."

"I'd do anything for you."

She gave him a bittersweet smile. "Even you, with all your money and power, can't fix this."

"I'd do anything for you," he repeated. "Are you listening to me?"

"I hear you," she said. "And I'm sorry I wasn't honest with you. But I didn't know myself. I was waiting to talk to my doctor the next morning. I just needed…a few more hours of normal. And I wanted to spend that time with you."

He accepted that explanation. But Tomas wanted more. And he wanted answers. "And now that you know what you're facing, why can't you still spend time with me? Why does that have to change?"

She shook her head. "I have to spend every minute of my spare time trying to get well, Tomas. I'm sorry but I won't allow you to go through that, and nothing you say is going to change my mind."

"Is that final?" he asked.

She looked away. "Yes."

Chapter Sixteen

ᥫ᭡

"Walk me home?"

Tomas nodded and waved to Alma and Winnie. "Of course."

"Let's go the back way," she suggested when they were out on the sidewalk. "Along the bayou."

"Okay." Tomas wanted nothing more than to humor her and help her, but his impatient nature wanted to grab her and kiss her and tell her to stop being so stubborn.

They might be wasting precious time.

But he strolled with her to the tiny park on the next block and took a left toward the Little Fleur Bayou. "I'm finally beginning to know all the waterways around here."

Her smile broke through the solemn look on her face. "It is confusing. But you said you used to live around here. Surely you remember all the bayous."

"We lived away from the water," he explained. "But back in the woods."

They turned back toward the bayou. Tomas focused on the crape myrtle blossoms and the sweet scents coming from the wisteria vines caught up in the old oak trees and magnolias.

"It's like one continuing garden back here."

Callie lifted her head to take in the fragrance in the air. "Yes. Don't you love it? I've been working on this little area for most of my life."

Tomas loved seeing her so content, the sun on her face, her hair tumbling out of her haphazard ponytail. She looked pale, but she also looked serene. "It shows."

When she opened her eyes and saw him looking at her, she shifted away and straightened her shoulders. "I've planted a lot of the flower beds along this path. "Iron weed and paperwhites, daylilies and rosemary, sweet olive and azaleas, and gardenias. I love the scent of fresh-blooming gardenias."

"I can see your hand on all of this," he said. "You are an asset to this town."

"I love this town."

They were almost to her front porch. Tomas stalled, held back. "Callie, we didn't finish our talk."

"I know." She motioned to the porch. "Let's sit here in the shade."

He followed her up the front steps and took a seat on an old bench, leaving her to sit in the white wooden swing. He knew her well enough to give her some space, at least.

Callie settled in the swing and pushed off with

one booted foot. "We can't be together, Tomas. We can't be an item. We can't be anything."

"Why not?"

She pointed to herself, a finger tapping her neck. "You know why. I'm sick again. Really sick. There are no predictions with this disease. We wait and we pray. I won't put you through that again."

He leaned forward, his eyes holding her. "You mean because of how my wife died?" He inhaled, thinking of his words to her on that Sunday in her papa's backyard. Realizing how what he'd said then might sound to her, he asked, "Why don't you let me decide that for myself?"

"It's my choice, my decision," she replied with a stubborn slant of her chin. "You don't need to decide."

Tomas wasn't used to being told he didn't have a choice. "So I have no say in this? I have to wait in the wings and hope you'll be okay? How does that make this better for either of us?"

She pushed at the swing, her eyes bright with doubt and anger. "It doesn't make anything better, but…we need to end things before we start them. You don't want to be a part of this, Tomas. You don't have any obligations here. I've seen what cancer does to a person."

He got up and stopped the swing with a hand. "Yes, and you've seen what it does to those who care about a person. So you think you've got it all figured out, right? You think that no man can handle breast cancer, right? That I can't handle this because of the way I felt watching my wife die?"

She looked both forlorn and formidable. "Yes."

"What about your father, Callie? He stayed with your mother. He never gave up and even today, he still respects her and loves her."

"And mourns her," Callie replied on a soft note. "Every day, Tomas. He mourns her."

Tomas sank down in front of the now-still swing, his hand holding tight to one of the weathered chains. "I don't plan on mourning you, if that's what you're worried about. I plan to see you alive and well…and with me. In my arms again, Callie. Do you understand?"

She shook her head. "*You* need to understand *me*. I can't do this. I can't hope that we can work this out. I don't have the answers. I can only tell you that I've been through this with another man and it didn't end well. I…I've come too far on my own to let that happen again. Especially with you."

Tomas stood, shock jolting through his entire body. "So you'll go through this alone, just to prove you can do it?"

"Yes." She stood, too. "I will get through this on my own. I can't hope for things I can't be sure of. I won't depend on…on you. I won't force you to stand by me. I'd rather do this my way, on my own, than to see you walk away."

"You're too stubborn," he said, for want of a better reasoning with her.

"You're too pushy."

He stared down at her, fire coursing through his veins. "I'll keep pushing, you can count on that."

She touched a hand to his arm. "I appreciate your concern and I'm thankful to know you, but…you don't have to prove yourself to me. I know you're a good man, Tomas."

"But not good enough to help you through this, right?"

"It's not you—"

"Don't say it. Don't tell me that it's all because of you and this noble idea that *you* have to prove something. I won't hear of that."

"Then we won't ever agree on anything."

"I suppose not," he said, turning to leave. Then because he was so aggravated and agitated, he pivoted around and pulled her into his arms and kissed her. When he lifted his head, he was rewarded with her gasp of surprise. But he saw the longing in her eyes, too.

He touched a finger to her cheekbone. "We can agree on that, at least."

He left before he got up the nerve to kidnap her and take her home with him forever.

Two weeks later, Callie knew she'd made the right decision. She had to keep Tomas away from the brutal reality of sickness and treatments and pain and agony. She was losing her hair now.

"I shouldn't be so vain," she told Alma while they both cried. "You have to help me shave my head."

Alma nodded, too choked up to speak. Finally, she took a deep breath and said, "We can have a shaving party."

"A what?"

"You know, invite people over, have cupcakes, laugh a little, cry a little. Clip and shave a little."

Callie grinned then sniffed. "I like that idea. But you don't have to go all noble and shave your head, too."

"Okay, I won't," Alma said. "But I want to support you in every way. What else can I do?"

"You're doing it," Callie replied. "You're here."

"Brenna will want to come to the shaving party," Alma said. "I'll call her. When do you want to hold this fancy party?"

Callie pulled at the broken strands of hair. "Soon."

"This weekend maybe?"

"Yes, Saturday?"

Alma nodded then said, "Oh, wait. That's the open house and picnic at Fleur House. We could do it Friday night."

"He's planned that already?" Callie asked, hurt that she hadn't heard more. But lately, she'd avoided the paper and the gossips mills, so she *wouldn't* hear more about Tomas.

That's what you wanted, she reminded herself. She'd chastised herself for even going out to see him in the vegetable patch. Her impulsive need to explain things to him that day had only made her want to be with him even more.

But that couldn't happen, especially now.

"Well, yes, he grudgingly planned the picnic," Alma said, her tone almost reproachful. "Spring's almost gone and summer is coming. Soon it'll be too hot to stroll around outside for hours and hours."

"I was supposed to help him plan that."

"We know. But you said—"

"I said I couldn't be a part of it, I remember."

"Brenna did most of the planning. And Aunt Serena, too. Papa has enjoyed seeing more of her."

Papa and Aunt Serena had visited her, and Nick's aunt had brought her a beautiful basket of all sorts of goodies—lotions, candy, books, candles and a beautiful colorful lap blanket.

"I'm missing out on everything," Callie said on a whine.

Alma came to stand by Callie and stared her down in the mirror. "It doesn't have to be this way, you know. The man is willing to do anything for you. I think he only agreed to the picnic because he's hoping you'll come."

"That's exactly why I can't let him get under my skin. He'd try to fix this and he can't."

"But you could spend time with him. He'd make you laugh, nurture you, watch over you. He's willing to do that for you, Callie."

Callie thought about that and wondered if her

sisters were tiring of always being there to help her. "Do you need a break?"

"Of course not," Alma said, her expression full of hurt. "How can you even say that? We all—and I mean *all*—Winnie, Mollie, the whole gang, Papa and the church ladies…we all want to help. Tomas is a part of that, or at least he'd like to be."

"But it's not as easy with him. I love each of you for helping but…I'm in love with him and I won't force him to do his duty out of sympathy. When I'm well—"

Alma's doubtful look shocked Callie. "You don't think I'll ever be well?"

"I'm praying for that every day," Alma replied. "I just wish you'd take advantage of the here and now, because we never know for sure about tomorrow."

Callie had heard that platitude one time too many lately. "As if I don't know that. I appreciate your advice, but…I just can't do it. I won't force the man to…feel pity for me."

"I don't think he feels pity," Alma replied. "I think he's in love with you, too."

Callie pulled at her hair and held up a wad in her hands. "This, Alma. This is why I can't allow Tomas back into my life. He shouldn't have to deal with this."

Alma looked skeptical but nodded. "Okay, I understand. But…you can at least go to the picnic and see the fruits of your labor. The gardens at Fleur House are first-class. Everyone's so excited about being able to see things up close. Think about it, honey. It would do you a world of good."

"I'll consider going," Callie promised. "I'd have to wear a mask to avoid catching anything. My doctor told me to be more careful about that. Being outside and with that many people." She shrugged, picturing herself in a scarf and a paper mask. Not a pretty sight. "It depends on how I feel that day."

But after Alma left, Callie stood there looking at her reflection and she knew in her heart that she wouldn't be at the picnic with Tomas.

She'd be just fine right here inside her little cottage.

Tomas went about his business. He held meetings at the shipyard and worked to keep as many people as possible on the payroll. His whole agenda had shifted and changed. The massive layoffs he'd planned had been turned to a few early retirements with severance packages and the promise of rehiring people soon.

He couldn't do all the things he'd planned to do.

Because he knew Callie wouldn't approve of that. She'd somehow changed him from the first moment he'd met her.

But she wouldn't let him love her. Not yet. Not now.

But soon, he thought. *Soon, Callie. Somehow.*

Today was the Fleur House grand opening and

picnic in the gardens. He planned to ask for a love offering to help Callie.

But he knew she wouldn't be here.

She who'd made these gardens beautiful again.

He wouldn't force her to come. He'd try a new tactic. He'd pray that she'd come. And he'd continue to pray to the God he'd scorned and shunned, to please spare her life.

As the day wore on and more and more people showed up to see his home, Tomas realized the people of Fleur had given him the best gift possible. They had accepted him as one of them, in spite of his initial reasons for coming to town, in spite of his bitter need for revenge on the family that had shunned him.

By the end of the day, he felt humbled and refreshed, less regretful and more hopeful. Everyone had seen his home, shared his food, played games on his fresh, new lawn and admired the gardens and landscaping that Callie had created out of weeds and shrubs and hard dirt.

But no sign of Callie. She wasn't going to make it today. She would probably never set foot at Fleur House again.

Tomas stood in the gazebo, waving goodbye as the crowd began to thin. When he saw Ramon Blanchard coming toward him, he stepped out and greeted him with a wave. "Hello there."

"Hello," Mr. Blanchard replied. "I need to talk to you." He glanced around. "Just you and me."

"Of course," Tomas said, wondering what he'd done. Mr. Blanchard looked so serious. Then Tomas's heart did a little jolt. Was this something about Callie?

"I have to get something outta my car," Mr. Blanchard said.

"All right. I'll be in the upstairs sunroom," Tomas replied. "It's quiet and private up there." And it made him feel closer to Callie.

He waited, every nerve in his body tingling with doubt and dread, until Ramon Blanchard came up the stairs and entered the coolness of the big oval-shaped sunroom.

He was carrying a flat square package wrapped in brown paper.

"What do you have there?" Tomas asked, motioning for the older man to have a seat.

Ramon sat down and stared out into the gloaming. "I'm a proud man," he began, "so dis is very hard for me."

"What is it?" Tomas asked, impatience to know pushing at him. Concern tearing at him.

Ramon ripped the paper off his package but held it away so Tomas couldn't see. But he thought he knew what Ramon held in his hands.

"The love offering," Ramon said, tears forming in his eyes. "I thought about giving money but dat'd be silly since dat's my daughter we're all fighting for." He sniffed and turned the painting around. "Dis is a treasure in our home," he began. "My Brenna painted it for her sister. Painted it for all of us." He stopped, sniffed, shook his head. "But rumor has it dat you tried to buy it off my Daughter Number Three."

Tomas held a clenched fist at his side, his own emotions drenching him in a burning heat. He nodded, swallowed. "I did, sir. Brenna refused to sell it to me."

"Dat's my girl," Ramon said, laughing through his tears. "She believes just like me dat you have to earn treasures here on earth."

"I understand," Tomas replied, fighting his angry pain. "So why do you want me to see this painting of Callie now?"

Ramon grunted and sniffed again. "I want you to make me an offer," he said. "I don't have a lot of money, but my girl needs my help. I told you I'm a proud man, so…I can't just outright ask for money, but…I know you want this painting and so… I'm willing to part with it as long as whatever you pay goes toward the love offering for my Daughter Number One. *Oui?*"

Tomas couldn't speak, couldn't move. He sat there staring at the old man holding the painting of Callie—Callie, laughing, smiling, out in a bright garden with butterflies around her. The painting Tomas had coveted from the first time he'd seen it.

"I can't buy your painting, Mr. Blanchard," he said, growling through his emotions. "But I will gladly help pay for Callie's medical expenses. I don't mind doing that at all. But you don't have to sell her portrait to me."

"Yes, yes, I do," Ramon replied. "I won't take money I can't repay. But I can trade something precious to me for money dat will help my daughter. It's the only way I can accept what you have offered." He looked down at the portrait he held in front of him. "Dis way, you can honor her and celebrate her life and I can keep my honor and know I did the right thing. You see, I'd rather have *her* alive and well in the flesh, than just an image of her hanging in my house. I got me enough of dat with her mama's face smiling down at me every day. I cherish her image, but…I don't want the same for my Callie. So please, just pay what you can and…help me get our girl well. Please?"

Tomas reached for the painting, took it and placed it up against a nearby table. Then he turned to Mr. Blanchard and helped the man to stand. "I'll be glad to make a donation to Callie's medical fund." He stopped, gathered his thoughts. "And when this is over and she's well, I'll return this painting."

Ramon gave him another solemn glance. "Me, I'm thinking we'll have to see about dat."

"Fair enough," Tomas replied.

They shook hands and Ramon nodded, tears streaming down his face. "I appreciate dis," he said, pumping Tomas's hand. "More than you will ever know."

"I know exactly how much it cost you to make

this deal," Tomas said. "And I promise you, you won't regret it."

"Just take care of her," Ramon replied. "Whatever it takes." With that, he turned and left, wiping his face with a handkerchief before he stepped back outside.

He'd never once asked how much Tomas was willing to pay.

That was because some things, Tomas knew, were priceless.

Chapter Seventeen

Callie loved the quiet beauty of the old cemetery where her mother was buried. She'd picked today, when she knew most everyone in town would be at the Fleur House picnic, to come and visit her mother's grave.

Her head wrapped in a floral scarf, she walked toward the rows of various mausoleums and tombstones and enjoyed the whisper of the afternoon wind lifting through the ancient mossed-draped live oaks and swaying palmetto palms. When she reached the Blanchard plot, she stopped and read the names of her grandparents and long-ago ancestors then found the crypt where her mother was buried.

Lola Calynda Blanchard. Callie was named after her mother, but no one had ever called her Calynda. Her mother hadn't liked that name, but her papa had insisted. So she'd given her firstborn the nickname of Callie and it had stuck.

Callie placed the fragrant white lilies she'd gathered from her yard against the warm stone, touched a hand to her scarf and smiled down on the verse from Proverbs etched in the marble. *A virtuous woman...her price is far above rubies.*

"You were priceless, Mama." She brushed away some lost magnolia leaves and wished she could give her mother just one more hug. She could almost smell the scents of almond cream lotion and vanilla flavoring.

Callie stood for a while, talking quietly. "I hope you'll help me figure this out. Tomas is a good man but he holds back. He wants to get closer to me, but he's still so distant at times. Maybe that's the real reason I can't let him into my life. I don't understand his life. And I'm not so sure I'll have a life much longer." She let out a long sigh. "Yes, Mama, my cancer is back. Can you believe that?"

Her mother would tell her to never give up. To stand tall and fight with all her heart. Cassie wanted to do that, but she was tired. She'd been through this fight before and she'd lost her marriage right along with her hair. How could she dare turn to a man she'd fallen for instantly and completely and ask him to stay by her side through the ugliness of cancer? She didn't even know if Tomas had staying power. She just knew he'd come into her life at the wrong time, or maybe at exactly the time she'd needed him. Only she didn't want to need him.

She didn't want to love him, but her treacherous heart hadn't given her a choice. She wondered what plan God had for her life. Was she destined to be alone and sick, dying and wishing, dreaming and accepting?

She thought about the one special night when Tomas had held her close and made her feel safe and secure and…equal. While she valued her freedom, she also longed for a strong marriage with a soul mate, with a man who could accept her hopes and her dreams and take her ups and her downs and still keep her on equal footing.

"I think he could have been that man, Lord."

Callie moved through the cemetery, looking at other tombs, reading names of people who'd gone before while she tried not to think about Tomas and what might have been.

A few rows over from her mother's grave, she found the Dubois mausoleum. Curious, she studied the tombs, reading each name and date. Then she strolled past the stone markers surrounding the designated Dubois boundaries. When she saw the name Delacorte on a tiny rose-etched headstone off to the side of the vast rectangular lot, she stopped and stared.

Rebecca Delacorte, beloved mother of Tomas Delacorte.

Callie gasped, put a hand to her mouth then glanced around. Tomas's mother was buried here in the Fleur cemetery? Callie remembered that he'd told her his mother had died when he was young but…they'd never discussed the details.

And even more puzzling, why was his mother buried so near the Dubois plot?

The sun hovered like a golden dome over the bayou.

Tomas waved goodbye to the last of his guests, memories of Nick and Brenna and Aunt Serena laughing and talking with Mr. Blanchard still fresh in his mind.

He'd missed Callie.

They'd all missed Callie.

"My sister is strong and brave," Brenna had said to the crowd when she got up to thank everyone for the love offering. "She will fight this and she will win."

Brenna had glanced over at Tomas, her eyes full of hope. Did she believe he could be strong and brave, too?

He could be, for Callie. He would be. He wasn't going to give up on her.

When he heard a car lumbering up the shell-encrusted drive, he turned with a frown. He was done with company for the day.

But when he saw Callie's old truck, his heart changed his mind and he instantly felt joy. Callie was here.

Tomas hurried to the truck. When he saw Pierre behind the wheel, disappointment hit him like a rogue wind. Then he saw Callie sitting in the passenger's seat.

"Callie?" he asked. "Are you all right?"

She nodded. "You can come back in an hour, Pierre. Thanks."

Pierre nodded, gave Tomas a questioning look and waited for her to climb down out of the truck. "I'll be here," he said in parting.

Tomas came around to help Callie. She was wearing a close-fitting straw hat. She looked so fragile he almost scooped her up in his arms. "Hi," he said, giving her a tentative smile. "You just missed the party. Everyone has gone home."

"I know," she said, her hand going up to her hat. "I…I need to talk to you."

Hopeful, Tomas pointed toward the gazebo.

She shook her head. "Can we maybe go inside? To the sunroom?"

Tomas nodded, talking to her the only thing on his mind.

He walked her through the house, his hand on her elbow. "Margie and Eunice went into town with Bob. They were delivering some leftovers to a couple of shut-ins."

Callie seemed to take in the house all over again, her gaze lingering here and there. "They're good people. We're blessed to have them as part of the community."

When they reached the sunroom, he asked, "Where do you want to sit?" He wasn't sure how to handle a quiet Callie.

"Here is fine." She chose a wicker chaise covered

with a floral cushion, centered in front of one of the big bay windows.

Tomas helped her onto the chaise and quickly offered her a yellow chenille throw. "If you're cold."

She settled back, then took off her hat, her eyes on him. She was wearing a scarf.

"Are you—" Tomas stopped, shook his head. "Your hair? You've lost your hair?"

She touched a hand to her scarf. "It started falling out. We had a shaving party."

"Excuse me, a what?"

"The girls and me, we had a shaving party. They helped me shave my head."

Tomas stared into her big eyes and saw the defiant light shining through. What could he say to that? How could he not grab her and hold her and… mourn the loss of all those luscious golden curls and waves? Her hair. He hated this. He hated cancer and illness and…death.

But he loved her. If he'd doubted that before, now, right now, he knew he loved her more than he'd ever imagined loving someone. And that scared him because he couldn't save her.

He had never felt so helpless and out of control.

"I can't say I've ever been to a shaving party," he blurted out. Then he looked away. "Would you like something to drink?"

"No."

She sat still. So still he had to turn back and stare at her. She looked gaunt and hollow-eyed. Some of her spark was missing, but she still shone a bright light on his life. "How are you?"

"Today is a pretty good day," she said. "Sorry I missed the picnic. I'm not supposed to be around large crowds—to avoid getting a cold or worse. I didn't want to have to explain anything."

He could understand that. People would stare, look sad. Mark her as almost-dead. But to Tomas, she was alive. Still very much alive.

"Callie…"

She glanced around then let out a gasp. "Where did that come from?"

Tomas looked over to the table to the right of her chair.

The portrait. He'd forgotten he'd left it here earlier.

"Tomas?"

"Your father brought it to me."

She looked shocked then her expression filled with anger. "Why?"

He sat down across from her. "Callie, he loves you so much. We had a love offering, to raise money for you. He offered me this."

"No," she said, hurrying to get up. "No. You can't just buy my health, Tomas. You shouldn't have taken this."

Tomas settled her back down. "I want to help and I have the means to do so." When she put up a hand to protest, he held tight to her arm. "I couldn't help my mother. I couldn't save my wife. I can help you. Don't deny me that, please. I won't keep the portrait, but I couldn't crush your daddy's pride. I intend to return it after you're well."

She sat there, silent and torn, her eyes misty with unshed tears. "I'm too tired to argue, but I don't like this."

"I understand, but your father expects you to get well. Let him hang on to that hope, okay? Let me hang on to that hope, too."

She stared out the window for a long time then surprised him with her next words. "Your mother is buried close to the Dubois lot at the Fleur Cemetery."

That comment knocked all the air out of Tomas's lungs. He sat staring at her, wondering how to explain. Wondering why he hadn't considered that she might find out. "Yes," he finally said. "Yes, she was buried there."

"Why?"

Tomas knew it was now or never. Callie expected nothing more than honesty. Pure honesty. And he hadn't been honest with her. "That's a long story."

"I have some time," she replied. She pressed her head back against the high back of the chaise. "Tell me."

Tomas stood. "I'll call Pierre and tell him not to come back. I'll take you home. If you want to hear my story, you need to stay here for more than an hour."

She held the chenille throw up against her, her hands clutching it. "Okay."

Tomas made the call then sat down across from her. "My mother lived down the road from this house when the last of the Dubois sons inherited the estate. There were three, but one died young and the other one left and went on to make his fortune in electronics. That left Gerard, and he took over when his father died. My mother worked all of her life and when she was in her teens, she'd occasionally do ironing and seamstress work for Mrs. Dubois."

Callie nodded, absorbing that bit of information. "So you've been here before?"

"No." He closed his eyes, prayed for courage. "It's a bit cliché, but when she was nineteen, Gerard Dubois had an affair with her and…she got pregnant. He was much older than her, but I guess they thought they were in love." He stopped, hung his head. "I'm…his son. His only son."

Callie's shocked breath brought his head up.

"Tomas, are you telling me you're the heir to Fleur House, to the Dubois fortune? Is that how you got your money?"

He laughed at that. "No. I'm not the heir. After my mother realized she was pregnant, she told Gerard but he kicked her to the curb and refused to help her or acknowledge me. He gave her a check and told her to stay away from his wife. He wanted no part of us, you see."

"Tomas—"

"No." He got up to pace around the long rectangular room so he wouldn't see the sympathy in her eyes. "No, *you* don't get to pity me. I'm okay now. I'm fine."

"Then why are you here?"

He sat back down, brushed at his hair. "My mother's parents turned her away. They're buried somewhere in that cemetery, too. After I was born, we moved about ten miles from here and got on with our lives. But we were so poor. Very poor." He took a breath, looked around at the grandeur of this house that had loomed like a dark shadow over his life. "I remember Christmases without food or clothing or toys. I never believed in Santa Claus and I gave up believing in God."

"Tomas—"

"You can guess the rest," he retorted before she could ask questions.

"Yes, I think I can," Callie replied. "You obviously worked hard and got a good education."

He smiled over at her, the bitterness he'd tried to hide bubbling up like quicksand. "I also got my real estate license and become successful in buying and selling commercial developments. I was the right-hand man to a very successful entrepreneur and when he retired, I took over."

"You didn't push him out, did you?"

He had to laugh at that. "No, but I guess people would assume that. He didn't have any children and…ironically…he considered me like a son."

Tomas stopped, shook his head. "Other than Bob, he was the only father figure I've ever had."

Callie played with the fringe on her blanket. "After your mother died, they took you in? Margie and Bob?"

He nodded. "My uncle and I had a fight. They let me live in their garage apartment, rent-free. I worked around the house and helped Bob at construction sites. I got scholarship money and used student loans to get an education. After I graduated from college, Bob introduced me to the world of real estate. That led to the job with the entrepreneur. So I owe a lot to them and him."

She inclined her head. "So…why did you really come back here?"

"Isn't that obvious, too? I wanted to live in the house I was denied. I wanted to be the wealthiest man in town, like my father before me."

She gave him a stare tinged with pity and realization. "And you wanted to shut down the company that the Dubois family still owns. You knew the shipyard was struggling so you bought it and then you moved in. You came after us, didn't you, Tomas?"

"Not you, no. There wasn't any *us* then."

She glanced at the portrait looming behind her. "There isn't any us now, either."

Tomas told her the truth. "I came here with a vendetta, yes. But…then I met you and your family and…started attending church…and all of that changed. My whole purpose shifted after I got to know all of you. Especially you."

Callie lifted up and swung her legs off the chaise. "Do the remaining Dubois descendants know who you are?"

"No one except Nick knows who I really am," he admitted. "There is only one Dubois left, and he's in a nursing home in New Orleans."

She stood up. "Your father? Gerard Dubois?"

"Yes."

"Does he know you're here?"

"No."

"But you made him an offer on the shipyard?"

"I had a representative make him a generous offer. The man is dying. He doesn't care about the Fleur Shipyard, and the people he hired to keep it going have done a bad job all the way around. He either had to sell it or go into bankruptcy, so I saw an opportunity and I took it."

"Is that how you do things?" She pointed to the portrait. "You see an opportunity and you just swoop down and…take what you think should be yours?"

Tomas turned to look at her and caught the whiff of her disdain. But she had a right to be doubtful.

"You don't know what my mother and I went through. We were always cold and hungry and we had very little help from anyone, not even the church. We were outcasts, Callie. No one wanted anything to do with us." He turned to stare out at the too-bright sunset. "I was the little boy who didn't have a father."

When he heard a rustling behind him, he turned to find Callie standing beside him. "I'm so sorry," she said, her tone full of compassion.

He looked out the window. "After she died, I came here to Fleur House and stood outside—right by that big double front door—and I shouted up at him, told him she was gone and it was his fault." Tomas sniffed, put his hands on his hips. "Before I could get back home, he'd had her taken away and the next thing I knew, her funeral was arranged and paid for and she was buried beside the Dubois lot. That is the only recognition she ever received from him." He looked out over the gloaming. "That is probably the only decent thing he ever did for anyone."

Callie came closer, tears moving down her face. "So you hate him?"

"Yes, yes, I do. I have hated him most of my life. I wouldn't have ever known him, except she talked about Fleur House all the time. I put things together, but I never questioned her. But I knew and sometimes, I wish I'd never known at all."

"Tomas." Callie stepped closer and placed her hands on his face, her fingertips brushing at his skin. "You don't have to seek revenge. You're safe now. You have everything a man could ever want, so you need to let this go."

Tomas put his hands over hers and brought their

joined hands down between them. "When I came here, I thought I'd finally achieved all my goals. I thought I did have everything I'd ever wanted. But…I don't have you. And I know I don't deserve you, so you need to explain something to me, Callie. Why are *you* here?"

Chapter Eighteen

Callie held on to his hands, showing him she still had the strength to fight for him, too. "Because I had to know the truth. I had to understand why you're so silent and standoffish at times and why you seem so determined to…fight against the world." She looked up and into his eyes. "Tomas, you might own Fleur House now, but you're still that little boy standing outside screaming at the man you hate. And until you let go of that image and that man, you will always be on the outside looking in."

Tomas pulled her close. "Not if I have you in my life. If I have you, Callie, I think I'll finally have a home."

Callie pulled away, shaking her head. "But that's not why I came here today. I only wanted to hear the truth, from you. And I find my picture sitting here in your house. Don't pin all your hopes on me, please. I don't think I can carry that weight along with everything else I'm dealing with."

Tomas touched a finger to her scarf. "Then let me carry you. Let me lighten your load. Just let me do that for you."

When she didn't respond, he said, "Now look who's being standoffish. I want to do this for you, Callie."

Callie wanted to be with him, but after what he'd just shared with her, she was even more convinced she'd made the right decision. Hoping he'd understand, she looked him in the eye. "You had a bad childhood and then you lost your wife to an overdose. Why would you want to go through this with me? Won't it just bring all that back?"

Tomas's eyes went dark at that comment. "Have you ever considered that by helping you through this bad time, I could possibly regain some compassion and…some redemption?"

No, she'd never considered that. His words echoed inside her head like a mantra. Was she being selfish by pushing him away? "I don't know," she said. "Tomas, this is not easy. You might become even more bitter and discouraged, and you know how I feel—"

"Yes, you like your independence. You're worried about all the baggage I brought with me. You think I'll wind up like your ex-husband, that I'll be disgusted and unable to handle this." He looked at her scarf then moved his gaze down her face. "You will always be beautiful to me, Callie. I don't need a portrait to show me that. I've been through the worst a person can go through and I've survived. I'm a fighter, just like you. And until I met you, I was willing to fight dirty. But I've changed. You have to believe that."

Callie saw the determination and resolve in his eyes. "I believe that. I do." She had to admit he'd been more open with her tonight than ever. "You've never talked this way before."

"I've never been confronted this way before, either."

She let out a chuckle. "Yes. You are a man of few words, but I can see you're beginning to trust me. I appreciate that."

"Then…just let me be your friend, someone you can turn to when your family begins to smother you too much."

That suggestion caught her heart. "You'd do that for me? Just let me be me, alone and…silent and… not having to answer questions or put on a happy face?"

"I'd do that for you," he replied. "I'd be honored to do that for you." He brought her close, gave her a soft smile. "Because I'm so very good at that myself, you see? I've had a lot of practice ignoring people, ignoring my feelings."

"You're right there," she replied, that familiar tug tightening around her heart. She laid her head on his shoulder and let out a sigh. "Don't hurt me, Tomas. I can't take that."

She lifted her head to look him in the eye. "All

this time, I've been telling myself I didn't want you to get hurt again, and I just realized I'm the one who's afraid. I've asked you over and over not to hurt me."

He gave her an indulgent smile. "You finally noticed that. But you have to see—I don't want to hurt you." He held her there while outside the dusk turned to a mauve-gray darkness that cocooned them. "I only want this."

Callie didn't speak, didn't protest. She closed her eyes and savored the quiet, enjoyed the scent of his aftershave, memorized the feel of his touch.

Seeing her portrait here had scared her at first, but now, being in his arms, it felt right. Papa was a wise man. And a very proud one. He'd sacrificed for her, in so many ways. Maybe giving Tomas that portrait was his way of letting her go.

"This is nice," Tomas said on a whisper.

"Yes." She let go and stood back. "I have to be sure, Tomas."

"We can take it slow, the way we talked about doing. That doesn't have to change."

She had a solid fear of being too weak to even smile at him, but…having Tomas near gave her something to fight for. But she also needed time. "Will you to take me home now?"

"Of course." He looked confused, but he walked her down to his car.

They rode in silence into town. When he pulled into her driveway, Callie glanced over at him and smiled. "Thank you, for telling me the truth. I understand now."

"And what do you understand?"

"That you've been wronged, hurt, abandoned. That you want retribution and…acceptance."

He nodded at that. "You can see the bitterness in me?"

She laid a hand on his arm. "No, Tomas, I can see the *goodness* in you. What you did for my papa today—I won't forget it. And because of that, I know you will be a blessing in my life."

He held her with his gaze, his dark eyes telling her much more than any confession ever could. "Thank you," he replied. "So…I can call you, come around now and then?"

"That would be nice."

"I'll take that for now," he said.

He got out and opened the door for her and walked with her up onto the porch. "Want me to come inside?"

"No." She laughed. "I'm pretty sure my sisters will be over here in about two seconds flat."

"They love you."

"Yes. They mean well."

"You have a good family."

Callie touched her lips to his face. "I'm always willing to share them, you know."

"I'll remember that."

He kissed her, a quick warm peck on her lips.

Then he walked back to his car and waited until she was in the house and had a light on.

Callie loved that he waited to see her safely inside, but she had to wonder if he'd stay here in Fleur in a house that he'd hated most of his life. He'd gone to a lot of trouble to finagle this whole thing—the shunned illegitimate son of one of the richest men in town coming back successful and bitter to take over what his father had denied him. A classic case of revenge and the need for retribution.

A classic case of how so many things could go wrong when everything should be so right.

And she was caught in the middle of it because her heart wouldn't let her turn away from this man.

Tomas needed her as much as she needed him.

But what would she do if Tomas suddenly decided he didn't want to stay here in Fleur with her?

He couldn't stay in Fleur House without Callie.

Tomas stood back to admire her portrait, which now hung on the wall over the sofa in the sunroom. No one else except Eunice and Margie had seen it, but now that Callie knew he had it, he wanted to display it. He didn't want to upset Callie, but he loved this painting. Loved being able to help her with her medical bills, even if she didn't like his generosity. She saw it as trying to buy her love, but he was trying to save her life. He'd pay whatever price he could for that chance. Only, he had no control over her health. No control at all.

But there were a few things he could work on. Now that she'd let him back into her life, he intended to show her he could be a better person. So he sat down and made a plan. He set up a conference call with Nick and a few of his other top advisors and assistants, explaining his new plan to improve the shipyard and make it better.

"We need to update the equipment, talk to union representatives and get their ideas for keeping the Fleur Shipyard viable. Nick, you will of course continue to update and improve the offices and the overall concept for the workplace. I also want to pursue more U.S. Navy contracts. If we can get commitments to build at least two ships, we can keep this shipyard up and running for several years."

Nick seemed surprised. "I thought you still planned to shut it down temporarily, or at least reduce production."

"New plan," Tomas had replied into the speakerphone. "More early retirements and severance packages. Less layoffs without reason. We want to make cutbacks, but let's look in other places."

"I like it," Nick replied.

Several of his other top advisors argued the point back and forth. Some wanted him to shut it down and call it a business loss and others encouraged him to make it an asset.

"I think we can agree we need to do our best to keep it open," he finally said. "That's the new plan."

He issued orders to Human Resources to find

maintenance workers, electricians and welders. He needed riggers and machinists and painters. He knew many of the townspeople could fill these positions, so he ordered a job fair to be held on-site within the next month or so.

The busywork kept him tied to his desk, but he made an effort to visit the offices Nick and Brenna had already started renovating. And he found time to call Callie at the end of each day.

Today, he looked over his desk and felt satisfied while he waited for her to answer. He'd accomplished something positive for a change. "So... how are you today?"

"Pretty good. Tired. I don't have an appetite."

"What would you like to eat if you had an appetite?"

"French fries, but I'm supposed to eat healthy. Although my doctor told me I need a variety of food since the chemo pretty much messes with my taste buds. Ice cream would be good."

"I'll bring you ice cream then."

Callie's sisters made sure she ate healthy, fresh foods so Tomas tried to honor that policy, too. He enjoyed picking her up on good days and bringing her out there for dinner in the gazebo. He picked beans and peas from the community garden and had Eunice cook them. He made Callie big, fresh salads and used lemon juice and olive oil to help keep her well fed. He studied books on how to deal with breast cancer and learned more than he ever wanted to know about the disease.

He watched over her all summer and thanked God for their quiet time here together. He offered to take her to her chemo treatments, but she always refused. Until one sunny morning when Alma called him, asking for help.

"I'm not feeling well and Callie has a treatment in New Orleans today. Papa is booked up with boat tours so I didn't even call him. He gets so emotional watching her have her chemo treatments. Brenna is in San Antonio. You're number four on the list. Can you take her?"

"Sure, but will she let me take her?"

"She will if I tell her so."

Callie didn't like this. It was one thing to sit with Tomas eating a bowl of pralines-and-cream ice cream, but it was quite another to be in a car with him, on the way to New Orleans for her treatment.

She glanced over at him, marveling at the strength in his fascinating face. "You understand this could take all day, right?"

"Right."

"And you know this means you'll miss a day of work?"

"I have my laptop and my cell."

"But…you must have a lot to do. I've heard from several people that you're really revitalizing the shipyard."

"Yes, I am doing that."

"So why are you doing *this?*"

Tomas shot her a quick gaze before he pulled out onto I-10, headed toward New Orleans. "I'm taking you to your treatment."

"I know that, but why… I mean…how?"

"Why? Because that's what a friend does for another friend. How? Because I have a car and I'm the boss so I can set my own work hours." He checked the traffic then patted her hand. "I don't mind doing this, Callie. Alma is busy with her café and she's pregnant. She needs a break every now and then."

"True, but I've told her that over and over."

"And Brenna and Nick are back and forth between work in Texas and work in Fleur, so they can't always be here to get you to New Orleans. And your daddy has obligations, too."

"He'd drop everything if I asked."

"Exactly. You don't ask. But people are more than willing to step in. I'm sure there is a long line right behind me."

She smiled at him, already enjoying being with him. "So how did you get bumped up to this new position?"

"I told your sisters to put me right below them in the pecking order. I'm Number Four on the list."

"Pretty soon my papa will be calling you Tomas Number Four."

She realized the implications of that statement, the intimacy of allowing him one of her papa's nicknames. Tomas gave her a look that told her he wanted that more than anything.

And maybe she did, too. She could at least imagine what it would be like to have Tomas in her life on a regular basis.

Someone to hold her hand when she was scared, someone to kiss her good-night and hold her tight. Someone—the one—who'd carried her back to her bed when she'd been so sick the night he found out the truth. Carried her and stayed with her, right there in the other room, most of the night.

Tomas Delacorte might present a moody, bitter face to the world, but the man had a heart of gold.

Callie saw that now, saw what most couldn't see.

She'd been ignoring the truth that was so obvious.

She had fallen for him in a love-at-first-sight kind of way, but she'd missed the most important thing about her feelings for Tomas.

Maybe God had sent Tomas here to be healed, but also to help her deal with being sick again. And possibly to give her something wonderful to remember, no matter how long she had to live from this day on out.

She laid her head against the seat, her smile filled with awe and discovery.

"You look so beautiful."

Callie lifted her head and looked into Tomas's eyes. She could see the bright spark of something real, something solid, there. Who was she to deny what was in her heart? Or what God had tried to show her from the beginning?

Tomas hadn't come into her life at the wrong time. He'd come into her life at exactly the right time.

Now if she could only live long enough to make the most of it.

Chapter Nineteen

Tomas gulped in another breath and tried to put on a stone-faced front. Watching the nurse inserting a slender tube into the port attached to Callie's upper chest made him want to kick and scream. But he had to be brave for Callie's sake. Because Callie sat there with a courageous smile and chatted with the nurse as if they were having a grand old time.

Tomas stared around the long room, noting several other people being given chemotherapy. Each patient had a comfortable chair and other necessities while cloth-covered plastic partitions gave them a bit of privacy.

The room was sterile and depressing in spite of the interesting artwork and smiling attendants, but the patients seemed to have high spirits. Or they were valiantly trying to have high spirits. How did they do that, day in and day out?

He waited and watched, checking on Callie several times between strolling outside to catch up on messages and answer the constant calls vibrating through his silenced phone.

"You don't have to stay with me," Callie told him. She had come prepared with a couple of romance novels and a devotional book to read, a magazine about interesting people and, of course, a gardening book.

"I don't mind sitting," he said. "If my phone would just quit buzzing."

"You're a working man." She smiled up at him, her floral scarf twinkling with sequined clarity. "I've been hearing all kinds of things about the shipyard."

He kept his stone face. "Such as?"

"That you haven't closed it down. That you didn't lay off the whole workforce. That you're working with management instead of firing all of them."

"Rumors, all."

"No, not rumors. You told me the truth, remember? You wanted to come here and shut that place down but...you didn't."

"Does that count in your book?"

"Yes. But I don't think you're doing that for me. I think you needed to do that for you."

Her eyes held his and Tomas had to hold back the urge to rush to her and pull her close. Callie, sitting there with no hair on her head and tubes coming out of her frail, pale body, her eyes even more vividly blue than before, her smile strong against her washed-out complexion, her body filling with a medicine that took the good away with the bad, a medicine that would make her deathly sick in the same way she'd been sick the night he'd found out.

Callie. Sitting there so strong and sure.

While he felt as if he were the one being pumped with toxins and bile because he couldn't do anything to help the woman he loved. He couldn't tell her he loved her because she was so afraid of hurting him, of hurting herself. Well, weren't they both hurting right now anyway?

"How do you feel?" he asked out of desperation.

"Okay. Like I'm floating, my insides tingling a little."

"Sorry I asked."

"You don't have to sit here and watch. Go take a stroll. I'll be a while longer."

"I don't want to leave you."

Ever.

"I'm not going anywhere." She glanced down at the open book in her lap. "Besides, you're making me nervous."

He stood, stretched, leaned down to kiss her. "I'll go check in with Nick and the ten other people trying to locate me."

"Good idea. And I'll go back to this good book I'm reading. I think it'll have a happy ending."

Tomas understood the undercurrents of that statement. He wanted *them* to have a happy ending, too. Maybe she wanted the same, but Callie couldn't be sure. No one could ever be sure. Until Callie, he hadn't really been a happy man. He thought he was getting there, though. Thought she could make him the happiest man in the world. But first he had to find a way to keep her healthy and safe. And…he had to find a way to let go of all the things he'd held so tightly—old hurts and hates, a grudge against a man he'd never known, and…vengeance against those he thought had hurt him.

Dear God, what do I do? I've always depended on myself. Now I have this mountain to climb, this obstacle that is bigger than any ship I've ever tried to build, any building I've ever had to reconstruct. How do I do it, Lord?

And how did the God he'd never considered as *his* allow him to even ask? What right did he have to pray to God when he'd turned away from any sort of faith because he'd seen the worst of human beings, even so-called Christians, when he'd watched his mother slowly dying of a broken heart?

"Where were You then, God?" he asked now.

Had the Lord been there beside him all along?

The truth echoed down this long, sterile hallway like wind passing through cypress trees. Had God been there?

He brought you to Margie and Bob. Gave you Eunice, too. He sent you to a man who trained you and sent you out to conquer the world. He made you a success and now—

And now, God had brought Tomas back to the one place that had molded him into a bitter, angry young man. God had put him into the path of the one woman who could change his hardened heart and make him feel alive again.

Maybe he was the one with the worst kind of cancer.

What would it feel like to let go of the bitterness? To finally give up on revenge and instead seek redemption and peace? What would it feel like to know that Callie respected him and understood him and forgave him of his shortcomings? That he didn't have to put on airs for her, or force major takeovers for her? What would it mean to lay down his head and sleep peacefully, without hurt or fear or torment?

Could God release him from all of that?

He stared at his phone, then he turned to stare at the doors to the big room where Callie sat, taking her medication.

How could he find any sort of peace if he didn't have her?

Callie settled back in the car, a lightweight sweater covering her in spite of the warm summer day. Glancing over at Tomas, she braced herself for the request she was about to make.

"Tomas?"

He glanced over at her, worry etching his expression. "Yes?"

"We should go and see your father while we're here."

"What?" Tomas gave her another glance, just a

shuttering of his eyes, and then headed out into the afternoon traffic. "I don't think that's a good idea."

"Do you visit him?"

"No."

"But…he's your father and he's dying."

"He wasn't much of a father when my mother lay dying."

"Did he know she was sick?"

His frown told her the answer before he spoke the words. "No. He didn't know anything about us because he didn't care about us."

"But if he'd known, I'm thinking he would have helped."

"He didn't bother checking."

"And yet, he gave her a decent burial with a rose-etched tombstone. That has to count for something."

"I don't want to see him, Callie. And I don't want to talk about this."

But Callie did want to talk about this. "Look, if I've learned one thing being sick again, it's that we can't take anything for granted. God brought you back to Louisiana for a reason. I think he wanted you to make peace with your father…before it's too late."

Tomas shot her an almost sheepish glance then turned his attention back to the road. "I've been wondering a lot lately about God and His moves and motives. I used to think He was cruel and un-caring, but…that was before I met you."

Pleased that he was thinking of his faith, Callie

still shook her head. "Don't pin all your hopes on me, Tomas. You need to be able to stand alone and face God. You need to give Him your heart before you even consider me."

"What does that mean?"

Callie wanted so much for this man. She wanted him to laugh and live and love and forgive. She wanted him in her life, but she wanted him to have God in his life first.

"It means you need to get right with God before things can be right between us."

"That's not fair."

"It is fair," she replied, her hand touching on his arm for a second. "Listen to me, okay? I don't know what will happen to me. I might beat this or…I might get worse. You've been through so much, never knowing your father, losing your mother and then watching your wife waste away. I don't want you to have to go through that with me. You need the Lord's protection and love in your life so you can handle things with a better perspective."

"So if I turn to God, I can deal with losing you? Is that what you're telling me, Callie?"

"Yes." There, she'd said it. "I think you need to be prepared."

He exited I-10 and hit the country road back toward Fleur. "I'm prepared to be with you for a very long time. I'm prepared to make you see that we belong together."

"And if that doesn't happen?"

"Then I'll deal with that…and God…in my own way."

"Tomas, you can't just deal with God on your own terms."

"Don't I know that."

Callie's heart thumped a warning that scared her. What if she ran out of time and Tomas was still enraged and caught up in the past? What if he couldn't let God heal him? What then?

She tried again. "You've been coming to church. Surely, that's helped you. You've changed since we first met. You're more relaxed now, more giving." Tears pricked her eyes; fatigue dragged at her body. "I know you're a good man. You've helped me so much."

He looked surprised at that. "How have I helped you?"

"Well, you've allowed me to take over your garden at Fleur House. Do you know what that means to me, to have free rein over such a big area, to plant to my heart's content in beds and areas I've created? To walk back through your yard and see the beauty that God allows me to be a part of? It's one of those things that rarely happen in someone's life. It was my biggest project ever, my biggest challenge. And I thought you were the worst of clients, but…you allowed that."

He shrugged, cruised around a curve. "I wanted the biggest and best garden in town."

"You wanted more than that. You wanted something beautiful to fill your empty heart."

"And I got you," he replied on a soft, sweet note.

Callie couldn't respond to that. She nodded and looked away, not wanting him to see the tears burning at her eyes.

When she felt his hand on hers, she turned to stare over at him. "Tomas…"

"I'm going to keep you, Callie. You're the only thing I want right now."

Callie didn't know whether to laugh or to cry. "I don't want to see you hurt. I can't bear that."

"I'll be okay. I promise." He went silent, his hand still gripping hers. "I've been praying a lot lately. And not just about you, although I pray every day that God will make you all better. But I've also been praying about myself, my life. I don't know if God is listening, but…I'm beginning to hope."

Callie couldn't hide her smile. "So all that protesting before was just bluster?"

"A little maybe. I'm still not so sure. This is new territory for me."

"You have a lot of people in your corner. God put them all there, you know."

"I've been thinking the same thing."

Callie watched the road, saw the water spreading out like a glistening gray blanket as they approached the Fleur Bayou Bridge. "Will you think about going to see your father?"

He shook his head. "That's one request I can't honor right now."

Right now.

But maybe later, Callie thought. Maybe he'd go and visit Mr. Dubois and finally put all of his torment to rest.

She'd pray for that to happen. Because she didn't think Tomas could truly understand love until he'd learned all about forgiveness.

Chapter Twenty

"I remember my wife being carted off to a rehab center. I would go and visit her, but I was never around when they gave her medication. I did sit in some therapy sessions with her, to try to save our marriage."

Tomas stopped rambling and glanced up at the man sitting across from him. Reverend Guidry was a big plump man with a perpetual smile. He'd stopped by to see how Tomas was doing. At first, Tomas had sat silent and determined behind the shield of his big desk. He didn't want to talk to a preacher about his personal problems.

He didn't want to discuss how Callie had urged him to go and visit his estranged father, either.

But this preacher, he was a tricky one. He'd waited Tomas out with an unflinching smile and a calm demeanor that was much worse than any torturous questions or probing persuasion. Now

Tomas seemed to be spilling every dark thought inside his head.

Reverend Guidry placed his hands together on his plump middle. "Did you want to save your marriage?"

Tomas thought about that before he spoke. Could he be truthful with a minister? "No. I mean, yes. Sometimes." He rubbed his tired, burning eyes. "Sometimes, I just wanted it over, one way or another."

The reverend gave him a sympathetic look. "And when it was over?"

"I blamed myself. I felt selfish and uncaring, as if I'd betrayed her. But our marriage was over long before she died. She was hard to understand, hard to live with. I tried but then I'm not easy myself." Tomas stared down at his desk calendar. "I stayed by her side because I hoped to get her well and then later...I thought I'd ask her for a divorce. I'm not proud of that, but it's the truth."

Reverend Guidry leaned forward. "And now, you're reliving some of those old feelings. But... Callie...well, she's a different kind of woman, isn't she?"

Tomas smiled at the way the good reverend had gotten right to the heart of the matter. "Yes, sir. I've never known anyone like Callie. She goes beyond being different. She dances in the rain."

"Oh, yes. Callie looks at each day as a new beginning while the rest of us dread getting out of bed at times."

Tomas nodded on that. "I can't stand to see her suffering."

Reverend Guidry nodded. "It's hard for those of us who care about her. That's why I came by to see you. Callie was concerned for you."

Tomas let out a brittle chuckle. "That figures. She's the one fighting cancer but she's worried about me."

"She thinks you're fighting your own battle."

"I've always fought my own battles," Tomas replied, the weariness of that admission sapping at his psyche.

The reverend did that silent thing again, his expression soft and sure.

Tomas wanted to sit and stare at the garden, but instead he let out a breath and spoke again. "Callie thinks I need to turn some of that over to God."

"How about *all* of it over to God?" Reverend Guidry replied, his fingers tapping softly on his blue jeans.

"That's a tough deal, Preacher."

Reverend Guidry stood, obviously proud of the work he'd done there. "The hardest deal to make but the one that brings the most reward."

Tomas stood, too. "I appreciate you coming by, but I'm fine. Callie doesn't need to worry about me. I just want her to be well again."

"We all want that," Reverend Guidry replied. "But we can't always get the things we want."

"And yet, I'm supposed to thank God for the time I've had with Callie."

"Every day, son, every day. We thank God even in times of trouble."

Tomas was still wrestling with that statement when Eunice came into his office later. "It's Wednesday night," she said. "Are you going to potluck and devotions at the church?"

Tomas glanced out the bank of windows behind his desk, the colors of Callie's garden shifting to soft, quiet shades of lush green and muted violet in the gloaming. He lived for potluck and devotions on Wednesday nights. "I hadn't thought about it."

"We're all going," Eunice replied. "Do you need anything before we take off?"

"No, go on and have fun. I'll decide if I want to come or not."

Eunice nodded, stood silent, her smile knowing and serene. "I'm glad the reverend came by today. We gave him a tour of the gardens."

"Did you?" Tomas stood, stretched. "We do have a showplace, don't we?"

"Yes. You should go out there and enjoy it yourself."

Tomas smiled. "I guess so."

But after Eunice left, he couldn't move. If he walked out into that beautiful garden that smelled like Callie, he'd probably find a rock to sit on and then he'd start ranting at the cruelty of life.

But then, as the reverend had reminded him, he needed to thank God for this suffering. After all, he was a blessed man in many ways. He had a beautiful old historic home and he had the most amazing garden in all of Louisiana, according to many people who'd seen it. And yet, he felt empty and drained and lonely. He felt defeated and helpless and inefficient.

"Maybe I do need to get some fresh air," he said to himself.

So he worked his way toward the back door and opened it to the humid summer night. He'd been here close to six months now, and while he'd become more relaxed with the people of Fleur, he still didn't feel as if he belonged. He was an interloper, sneaking around in this house full of lost memories. He wondered what his father had said or done in the office that was now his. He thought about how his life might be different now if he'd grown up here at Fleur House. Would he be running the shipyard, the heir to the Dubois legacy? His father had no other children. Only distant relatives who were just waiting for him to die.

Isn't that what you're doing, too? Waiting for your father to die?

Was that just? Was that in God's plan?

Tomas made his way to the gazebo, memories twinkling around him like fireflies. He stared out into the dusk, thoughts of Callie with him here. He'd held her close on that night all those weeks ago, held her and fell in love with her all over again. He'd fallen for her on sight, but getting to know her had only added to that first foolish infatuation. The infatuation had turned into something real, something life-changing.

Are you ready to change?

That doubt again.

Tomas stared at the gazebo and saw the shadows of his hopes, the scents of gardenia, jasmine and honeysuckle intoxicating him with dreams. Somewhere off in the swamp, an owl hooted to the moon. The wind played a soft dance across the trees, bending the Spanish moss into silvery threads of lace.

And he missed her.

She wants you to change, he reminded himself. *Do you want to change for her?*

Tomas wanted her to love him. That much he knew.

But was he willing to change in order to have that love?

Callie sat at a far table near the back door of the fellowship hall. Partly in case she couldn't make it through dinner, but mostly to avoid germs. Although she'd been feeling a little under the weather all day, Alma had suggested she come over to the church for the meal, and her sister had fixed her a plate with protein and healthy foods—baked chicken and brown rice, leafy greens and a fruit and yogurt parfait Alma had created just for Callie.

"Greek yogurt, blueberries, strawberries—lots of super foods," Alma had announced with a hopeful smile.

Everyone was trying to save her, Callie thought, her stomach already churning, her skin clammy and hot. But she nibbled at the food in front of her because she wanted her body to stay healthy. And she wanted to keep fighting against the constant fatigue and the dark fears clawing at the joy in her heart. She wouldn't give in to the fear. There was no fear in loving Jesus. She'd be safe, no matter in this life or in heaven. She sipped her ginger tea and smiled and chatted through her paper mask.

Don't think like that, she told herself. She wanted to survive, to see the sun rise over her nursery, to hear the birds sing in her garden. To dance with Tomas again in the gazebo. She would survive this.

She looked up and saw him standing across the room. Callie's heart did a bump, bump, bump against her chest. Tomas was here. She hadn't been to Wednesday potluck in a while, but she'd heard he came often. He saw her and started walking toward her.

Callie felt clammy all over again, her vision blurring, a light-headed dizziness causing her to feel not so good. Okay, so she was glad to see the man but this was ridiculous. Hot chills laced her spine, tightening against her skin until she couldn't breathe.

Alma rushed over to her. "Are you okay? You look so pale."

"I don't know," she said, putting a hand to her forehead. "I feel a little hot. Is it hot in here to you?"

Alma placed her palm on Callie's forehead. "Your skin is warm. You might have a fever."

"I guess I am in love then," Callie quipped. "Tomas is here."

"Are you kidding me or do you really feel bad?" Alma asked in a curt tone, her concerned gaze moving over Callie's face.

Callie tried to smile, tried to nod. "I…I don't feel so great either way." She tried to stand but had to grab the table. "I mean, I really don't feel so good."

Alma held Callie, an arm wrapped over hers. "I shouldn't have talked you into coming over here tonight. I'll take you home. But, Callie, you need to call your doctor."

Callie tried to nod, tried to respond, but her body was on fire and her stomach shifted and roiled with each step toward the nearby door. "I'll be fine. Just need to lie down awhile. Guess I'll go to bed early."

And then strong hands took over where Alma left off. She looked up and into Tomas's face and felt herself go weightless as he lifted her into his arms. "I'm taking you home," he said into her ear. "Just hold on. It'll be okay."

Callie stared up at him, grabbed his shirt collar. "Don't take me home. Take me to the hospital."

Tomas sat along with Callie's family in the large E.R. waiting room at the New Orleans hospital where he'd brought her two hours ago. It was late now and the E.R. had settled down.

But his heart and his stomach were both still bouncing and shifting. He put his head down, his hands templed at his knees.

He didn't know how to pray.

Mr. Blanchard walked over and sat beside him. "Dis is de same hospital where we brought her mama."

Tomas sat up and saw the pain in Ramon Blanchard's dark eyes. He didn't ask the obvious. Had Lola died here? He didn't ask because he didn't want to put that into words—nothing about death should be said tonight. Callie wasn't going to die.

"Febrile neutropenia," Alma said from her spot across the aisle. "That's doctor-speak for she's taken on an infection somehow. But she's been so careful. She stayed away from the picnic at Fleur House—" She stopped, gave Tomas a wide-eyed glance. "She didn't want to make a big deal out of it, but the doctor told her to stay home."

Tomas wondered what else they hadn't told him. But then, he wasn't really family. Yet. "But will it go away?"

Alma nodded. "We hope so. They'll treat her with

certain medicines and antibiotics. Hopefully, that will zap it."

Hopefully. Tomas got up and paced. Julien passed him with fresh drinks—water, coffee, soda.

"Did you call Brenna?" Papa Blanchard asked.

"Yes, Papa," Alma replied. "She's waiting to hear the latest. She sends her love."

"I can have them flown home," Tomas offered. "Brenna and Nick."

"Thanks, but not yet," Alma replied.

Tomas was beginning to read the unspoken things. *Not now, Tomas. It might get worse. Much, much worse.*

He hated death. Hated waiting in hospitals. But he also remembered wishing when he was young and helpless and afraid that he could take his mother to a nice, clean hospital. He hadn't been able to do anything then and surprisingly, he couldn't do much for Callie now.

He'd worked hard, so hard that he'd forgotten how to do anything else, just so he'd never be in that situation again.

And yet, here he stood, supposedly rich and powerful and ruthless at times, but right now, completely helpless and poor in spirit.

Callie woke out of a lace-covered sleep. She tried to sit up, tried to remember where she was. Glancing around, she realized she was at the hospital. When she noticed someone covered in scrubs asleep in the chair next to the window, she blinked and tried to focus.

"Tomas?"

He jumped, his head lifting. "Are you okay? Do you need something?"

"Tomas, what are you doing here?"

He pushed at his dark hair, shook his whole body awake. "They moved you to a room. I wanted to stay."

Stay.

He'd stayed with her. Again.

"Where are Alma and Papa?"

"Out in the waiting room. They came in to see you, but you were sleeping."

"What time is it?"

He glanced at his watch. "Three in the morning."

"You need to go home."

"I'm not leaving."

Callie lay back, too exhausted to argue. "What's wrong with me?"

"You have a low-grade infection." He pointed to her left hand. "You have a cut on your left palm. They think it started there."

Callie lay still, closing her eyes. "I worked in my back garden last week. I didn't wear gloves." Her voice shook. "I got a little prick from a thorn somehow. Tomas, I didn't wear gloves."

He got up and came to the bed, his gaze telling her he wanted to touch her. "It's okay. You'll be okay."

"I knew better," she said, tears blurring her eyes. "But I wanted to feel the dirt in my hands. I miss that, miss the sun on my face. Miss the rain on my skin. I…I shouldn't have done that. I don't know what I was thinking."

Tomas took her hand and held it in his. "You were being you, Callie. It's okay."

Callie wanted to believe him, but she was so tired. "I planted a Gerber daisy. I love Gerber daisies. They were blooming a bright red. For my back porch."

"I'm sure they're very pretty."

"Someone will need to water them for me."

"I'll make sure your daisies are taken care of."

"And Elvis. He'll wonder where I am. He likes to go out early in the morning."

"I'll make sure Elvis is safe."

She stared up at him and saw the anguish he was trying so hard to hide. Callie wanted to kiss Tomas, to hold him, to tell him that she loved him so much. But…she might not be able to hold to that promise. She wouldn't tell him that, not until she could stand on her own two feet and hold him in her arms.

"You should go," she said, anger and frustration coloring her tone. "I don't need you staying here all night. I have nurses, and the doctors probably don't even want you in here."

"I'm not leaving."

"You have to go and check on Elvis."

Tomas let out a sigh. "I will do that, and I'll water your daisy, but later."

"And you'll make Papa and Alma go, too."

"Yes. Now rest."

She closed her eyes. But she was wide-awake now. "Tomas, will you do me one more favor?"

He smiled a tired, sleepy smile. "Anything."

"Go and see your father."

Chapter Twenty-One

❧

Tomas stood at the double doors of the long elegant hallway, his gaze centered on the door at the end of the hall. This would be the longest walk of his life.

But he'd promised Callie.

She was weak and in pain, the infection taking over her body. And she'd asked this one favor of him.

It didn't matter that he'd quietly brought in specialists and experts to save her. It didn't matter that Tomas had prayed, had thought over his own miserable life. It didn't matter that he loved her and wanted a chance with her.

It only mattered right now that he had to do this for Callie. To tell her he'd done it for her.

Do it for yourself.

Tomas ignored that voice and started walking the long, tiled hallway. His gaze swept over the tranquil paintings by local artists, some by the residents here. Nice and probably good for morale. Pretty and pleasant in spite of the antiseptic smell. This wing was new and clean and soothing.

He should know. His money had built it.

At the time, he'd thought the joke was on his dying father, Gerard Dubois. Now, ha-ha, the joke was on him. He couldn't save any of them, especially himself.

Callie thinks you're salvageable.

Maybe God thinks you're worth saving, too.

He stopped at the set of wooden doors that would take him into his father's suite of rooms. Tomas swallowed, closed his eyes and knocked.

A private nurse he'd interviewed and hired but only spoken to on the phone since, opened the door, her gaze going wide at seeing him here. "Hello, Mr. Delacorte."

"Hello, Beth. How is he?"

"Restless. It's hard to know if he's in the here and now or…reliving a long-ago memory."

Tomas thought that sounded a lot like his own days, too.

He nodded to the nurse and walked past the den-and-kitchen combo to the big bedroom at the end of the suite. A set of bay windows offered a view of the secluded courtyard full of azaleas and dwarf magnolia trees. A palm tree swayed in the wind near a fountain that constantly flowed in a soft, melodious pattern down into a small lily pond.

If only the old man in the bed could see that view.

Tomas stopped at the foot of the bed and stared

at his father. He could leave now and he would have fulfilled his obligation. He'd come here and he'd seen his father.

It was enough for him.

But not for Callie. She demanded all of him. She wanted all of him for God, too. Grace, love, hope, redemption. Those were Callie's whispered words to him.

"Go, Tomas. Go and see him and forgive him before he dies. It's not for his sake. It's for your sake. You can't know love or hope or redemption until you've given someone else the grace of Christ. It will heal you."

Tomas closed his eyes, determined to keep the tears at bay. He didn't need healing. He needed to understand.

"What are you doing here?"

Startled, he opened his eyes to stare into his father's face. And saw his own reflection there.

"I...wanted to see how you're doing."

"I'm dying. What's to see?"

"Are you being treated well?"

"Better than most. But if I could, I'd get out of here and never come back."

Tomas had once relished this gilded prison. When he'd first heard the old man was living in a dirty corner of an unkempt nursing home, he'd felt a sense of vengeance followed by a twinge of humanity. So he'd visited other retirement centers and found this one and moved the old man here. Then to really turn the screws, he'd built a whole new wing in his father's name. After he'd had Gerard Dubois settled nicely into his new suite, Tomas had introduced himself. Just to show the man that he was now a prisoner in his son's life.

That meeting had not gone over very well.

His father had not been repentant.

Now he had to wonder why he should show this selfish man any mercy.

"What do you want?" Gerard asked through a gurgling cough.

Tomas wondered that himself. "I don't know," he said, honesty his shield. "I've met a wonderful woman and I'm in love with her, but she's gravely ill."

"Your track record with women isn't so great is it, son?"

Tomas almost shouted "Don't call me son," but instead he laughed. "I guess not."

His father gazed up at him with sunken eyes. "So you're in love and you've come here to gloat? Or maybe you've come here to tell me to just go on and die?"

"I'm in love and I came here because she thought it might help me if I…finally forgive you."

His father stilled on the bed, his expression full of shock and hope. "Can you do that?"

"I've been trying to do that for most of my life, sir."

Gerard grunted, clutched at the covers. "Me, too,

son. Me, too." He cleared his throat and stared up at the ceiling. "I don't know how to explain what I did to your mother and you. I was young and married and stupid. I had this image to uphold, you know."

"Yes, I know all about your image."

"You've become a man of means and I have to say, while I didn't have anything to do with it, I'm still proud of you."

Once, long ago, that kind of recognition from his father would have pleased Tomas. Now it only left him empty. "You had nothing to do with my life, so you don't need to praise me now."

Gerard reared up then fell back against the pillows. "I take that back. I had everything to do with your life. You just didn't know it. Margie and Bob? I asked them to watch after you and your mom. Tried to pay 'em but they turned me down flat on that."

Tomas couldn't speak. "I don't believe you."

"I don't care what you believe. It's too late for convincing now, anyway. The man who took you under his wing and gave you a job in real estate? I knew him from some early dealings. I had him reporting to me on your schooling and your salary, and while I never had to pay your way, I was always there waiting in the wings. Watching out for...my only son."

Tomas moved toward the bed, ready to lash out. But when he saw a single tear slipping down his father's wizened face, he stopped and thought of Callie. He should be with her right now. Not with this man he didn't even know. So he softened his reaction and planned to end this and hurry back to her.

"Why didn't you ever tell me? Why didn't you acknowledge me?"

Gerard shook his head. "I was too proud and stubborn. But…that's the past. I'm glad you're in love. Make the most of it. Go, and don't worry about me. I've more than paid for my sins."

Tomas wondered about that. "Have you?"

Gerard let out a brittle cackle. "Look at me. Alone and dying. If you hadn't come along, I'd still be in that cesspool of a nursing home. My wife hated me and we couldn't even have children. She died hating me. What do you think? Haven't I paid for what I did to you?"

"I don't have the answer to that," Tomas said. "But…I want to have a good life with Callie Blanchard. I love her. I want her to get well and marry me. So I'm here to say I forgive you. I forgive you for what you did to my mother and me." He stopped, a great breath of relief washing over him. "I forgive you."

Gerard blinked back more tears then reached out a shaking hand to his son. "I've waited to hear that since the day you were born."

Tomas took his father's hand, his own tears cooling his heated skin. He stood there, holding his father's frail fingers in his palm until Gerard had drifted back to sleep. And then, for a while longer.

* * *

Callie smiled at the nurses hovering around her. "I'll be okay, I promise. I'll wear gloves and masks and a full bodysuit if I can avoid this again."

The orderly helping her into a wheelchair laughed out loud. "Miss Callie, we're sure gonna miss you. You've always got that smile. We need that smile around here."

Callie grinned and pointed to the Gerber daisy sitting on the windowsill. It was blooming to beat the band. "I'm leaving my flower with y'all. Think of me when you see it."

They all gushed and giggled.

"I'm putting it at the nurses' station right now," one of the nurses stated. "You have a gift with gardening, Callie."

"I do," Callie said, in awe. "I'm blessed."

One of the nurses turned when the door opened. "You sure are, honey."

Callie saw Tomas standing there with more flowers. No roses, of course, but a bright bouquet of wildflowers.

"Hi," he said, slipping into the room. "Ready to go home?"

"Yes." She thanked God she was better, so much better. "Are you ready to take me home?"

"Very." He handed her the flowers then leaned down to kiss her. "I love you."

"I love you, too." She could tell the difference in him almost immediately. "How's your father today?"

Tomas shook his head. "Stubborn, contrary, but… he's holding his own."

Callie didn't press for any more details. She only knew that Tomas and his father had made their peace and now, Tomas seemed younger, stronger, more happy than she'd ever seen him. He'd come to her late one night and told her that he'd talked to Gerard Dubois. He'd cried and they'd prayed together, thanking God for this grace. Then Tomas had told her he loved her.

"Plain and simple, like that?" she'd asked.

"Not so plain and surely not so simple," he'd replied. "But yes, just like that. From the moment I saw you out in my garden."

Now, she kept smiling over her shoulder as Tomas followed the wheelchair out into the bright morning sunshine. Out at the car waiting at the entrance, she saw her papa with Aunt Selena, Alma, Julien, Brenna and Nick. Her family was waiting for her.

She turned back to Tomas and nodded. "My life is complete."

He leaned down again and kissed her. "Not quite. You still have to marry me."

And there with her family surrounding her, Callie watched in awe as Tomas got down on one knee in front of her, a tiny black box in his hand. "Will you marry me, Callie?"

Callie stared at him then glanced at her waiting family. The tears in her sisters' eyes caused her to shed a few. But when she saw her proud, sweet papa wiping at his nose, she knew she couldn't be any more blessed. The infection was gone and her doctors had assured her she was on the mend. Her cancer was in remission. She'd beat it once again. Now she only wanted to be with Tomas. "I will. I will marry you."

The nurses and the orderly clapped and whooped while Tomas put the sweet solitaire on her finger and kissed her. "Now we can take you home," he said.

The next spring

"You may kiss the bride."

Tomas grinned at Reverend Guidry then turned to pull Callie into his arms. She felt so solid and sure, healthy again and strong again, his forever.

When he lifted his head, her smile shone like the sun and warmed him deep inside his heart, in that place that had hurt for so long. The place that she'd helped to heal.

All around the gazebo, their family and friends clapped and cried and hooted their approval, his father, frail but determined in his wheelchair with his nurse Beth watching out for him, included.

The beautiful spring day looked ready-made for a wedding, with lush, white Casablanca lilies scenting the air in the garden that Callie had built and nurtured in the same way she'd shaped and nurtured him.

Tomas kissed her again as they moved down from the ribbon-bedecked gazebo and followed the trail of gardenia petals to the wide terrace on the back of the house to enjoy all kinds of food and the wedding cake. Alma and Brenna traipsed around in their floral bridesmaid dresses while Nick and Julien served as best man and groomsman, respectively. Mrs. LeBlanc held her new grandson, Jules, but Alma patted her four-month-old and tugged at his fuzzy blue socks as she walked by.

Tomas didn't pay much attention to the Zydeco music or the food or the many happy people mingling in his garden. He couldn't take his eyes off the bride.

Callie, in her mother's wedding gown with a simple tiara of baby's breath as her veil, her chin-length bob of newly grown hair curly and carefree. Callie, laughing and tanned, smiling and in remission from her cancer.

Callie. His at last.

After everyone had left and his bride was huddled in a corner with her sisters, Tomas turned to find Ramon Blanchard walking toward him.

"Mr. Blanchard," Tomas said with a handshake. "How are you, sir?"

"Call me Papa," Ramon said, his dark eyes centered on his three girls. "I came to say I want to thank you for all you've done for my Callie."

Tomas looked down, embarrassed. "You can have

her portrait back, you know. I don't expect you to allow me to keep it."

Ramon shook his head. "You don't understand, *mon ami*. I don't need de picture to know my daughter is beautiful and precious."

"I don't, either," Tomas admitted. "I have the real thing."

"Yes, you do at dat," Ramon said on a roll of laughter. "And I expect you paid dearly for that privilege. Don't ever take it for granted."

"Never." Tomas watched as Callie laughed and waved to them. "But about the portrait…"

"Keep dat, too. I can never repay you for all you've done, but if you take good care of her, dat's payment enough, *oui?*"

"Oui," Tomas replied, his eyes on Callie. "Now I have a new work of art."

Ramon laughed again. "Gonna be a mighty interesting time at your house, I reckon."

Two hours later, Callie and Tomas were back in the gazebo watching the sun setting over the bayou.

He held his bride close, the scent of her distinctively floral perfume tickling at his nose. "You are a beautiful bride."

"Thank you. I felt beautiful today. A perfect day."

"The best," Tomas agreed. "Callie, are you sure you want to live here?"

She turned to stare up at him. "Are you sure you want me to live here?"

"You're my wife, so yes, I'm sure."

"We could renovate that old carriage house up on the road," she said, grinning. "It's smaller and covered in kudzu and bramble, but I've always thought it would make a pretty English cottage."

Tomas threw back his head and laughed out loud. "You have Fleur House, but now you want an English cottage?"

"I don't have Fleur House. It belongs to all of us."

He understood what she was saying. "But…what about children?"

"I like children."

"I mean, we'd need more room."

"They'd have all of this to run around on. I can keep a watch over the gardens and we can open the house for parties and tours. Maybe even weddings."

"You've thought this through, haven't you?"

She nodded. "But…renovating the cottage will take time. For now, we have our honeymoon to consider."

He nodded at that. "Yes, and I do believe my bride requested spending our first night together right here at Fleur House."

"I do believe you are right," she said. "But right now let's watch this sweet sunset."

But when they glanced back, the skies to the west had turned dark. A strand of lightning blazed the sky then thunder boomed loudly overhead.

"Never mind that," Tomas shouted. "Let's get you inside."

But he knew with the first fat drops of rain that his bride wasn't ready to go inside. So he watched and laughed and thanked God for her.

While she lifted her arms to the sky and danced in her mother's wedding gown.

In the rain.

When she turned and motioned for him to join her, Tomas gave in and gave away his heart. He ran out and grabbed her close, and together they laughed up at the sky.

Then he lifted his bride, wet skirts and all, into his arms and carried her into their home.

* * * * *

Dear Reader,

This story has to rank as one of my favorites (as much as one can love one's own work, that is). But I knew the day I met Callie that she would require a special man in her life. Callie was content being single and alone, but she dreamed of a family of her own and secretly longed for someone to love. Tomas was a tortured soul bent on getting even with the people who had scorned him. So sunshine and light meets darkness and despair and together, Callie and Tomas find a good balance of faith and love and forgiveness.

I hope you enjoyed this final installment of my bayou series. I might revisit Fleur, Louisiana, one day and see what's happening with the Blanchard clan. I sure will remember these characters for a long time to come. Thanks for taking this journey with me.

Until next time, may the angels watch over you. Always.

Lenora Worth

Questions for Discussion

1. The theme of this story is forgiveness. Do you find it hard to forgive someone from your past? How have you handled this?

2. Callie has a sweet spirit and an outgoing nature that charms people. But Tomas was hard to charm. Do you think she was being vain in wondering why he didn't like her? Did she handle things in a good way?

3. Tomas had a lot of bitterness to deal with. Have you ever felt this way? Do you tend to hold things inside or open up and let go?

4. In spite of his chaotic childhood, Tomas had a love of art and beauty. Do you think this is why he was so attracted to Callie? How did getting to know her help him to slowly change?

5. Callie's attitude was one of faith and hope. Tomas had an attitude of doubt and despair. Even with all his money, he couldn't be positive. Have you ever felt this way in spite of being blessed? Do you sometimes doubt your faith?

6. Callie loved the outdoor world and growing things. But she was also sick and had to stay

inside. How do you think this changed her attitude? How did her faith help her?

7. Tomas had lost his wife to addiction and pain. Is this why he was afraid to love Callie? Or did he just have a distrust of faith?

8. Tomas told Callie he'd stayed by his wife until the end. Why was it so important that she understand this about him?

9. Callie didn't want to be a burden or obligation to her family or Tomas. Why did she try to hide her illness from him? Why did he fight to save her, and how did that fight change him?

10. The Blanchard family was very close and very strong in faith. Tomas had no one and his faith was shaky at best. Have you ever invited someone like that into your family?

11. Callie's sisters rallied around her to help her get well. Do you know people who'd do the same for you? Have you ever dealt with a health crisis?

12. Tomas had to learn to trust everyone around him. How did Callie help him do this? Why did she insist he go to his father and forgive him?

13. Gardening is a pleasant and comforting pastime for many. Why is it so true that we are closer to God in a garden?

14. Callie found solitude in her work and with her dog, Elvis. Together, the two gave her a sense of security. How did Tomas mess with that? Why did she resist him at first?

15. Tomas fell for Callie when he saw her dancing in the rain. But he had to get to know her before he could act on his feelings. Why is it important that we get to know people before we judge them, good or bad? Have you ever misjudged someone based on first impressions?

LARGER-PRINT BOOKS!

GET 2 FREE LARGER-PRINT NOVELS PLUS 2 FREE MYSTERY GIFTS

Love Inspired

Larger-print novels are now available...

LILPDIR13R

ReaderService.com

Manage your account online!

- Review your order history
- Manage your payments
- Update your address

> *We've designed
> the Harlequin® Reader Service
> website just for you.*

Enjoy all the features!

- Reader excerpts from any series
- Respond to mailings and
  special monthly offers
- Discover new series available to you
- Browse the Bonus Bucks catalog
- Share your feedback

Visit us at:
ReaderService.com